In the Sheikh's Grasp

Sands of Passion, Volume 1

Amara Holt

Published by Amara Holt, 2024.

Copyright © 2024 by Amara Holt
All rights reserved.

No part of this book may be reproduced, distributed, or transmitted in any form or by any means, including photocopying, recording, or other electronic or mechanical methods, without the prior written permission of the author, except in the case of brief quotations in book reviews.

This is a work of fiction. Names, characters, places, and incidents are the product of the author's imagination or are used fictitiously. Any resemblance to actual events, organizations, locales, or persons, living or dead is coincidental and is not intended by the authors.

PROLOGUE

Helena

"Wake up to reality, Helena!" I roll my eyes at Vitória's words.

"And did I ask for your opinion?" I ask, putting my notebook into my backpack. As soon as I finish, I grab the strap of it as I stand up.

"Do you think a bland Brazilian like you has a chance with an Arab? Wake up to life! You'll never even leave Brazil."

If it weren't for the fact that she hates me, I would be offended by her words, but Vitória has never accepted that I keep the highest grades and couldn't care less about the boys in the class, including her crush who's always on my case.

I grab my phone from the desk, turn my back on the girl, and leave her talking to herself.

As I pass through the door, I see my sister holding hands with her current boyfriend.

"Who's the flavor of the week?" Fernanda asks.

"Vitória, as usual." I roll my eyes.

"Again? If you want, I can take care of her," she says, letting go of her boyfriend's hand and dismissing him.

"It's fine, I don't mind." I shrug.

"I wish I had your calm, Helena. What did she say?" she asks as we walk towards the exit.

"She saw my notes about the seven United Arab Emirates in my diary."

"Sis, you're so *nerdy*. Don't forget you're only fifteen. You need to go out and meet different people. Get that fascination with sheikhs and all that stuff out of your head..." She gestures with her hand.

"I believe I was born into the wrong culture."

"Sure, my dream is to be bossed around by a man. We are very different from them, sis," Fernanda concludes with irony.

In part, my sister is right, but that doesn't erase the fact that one day I want to visit one of the Emirates. All that luxury, a parallel universe, it almost seems like they live in another world.

We leave school, the late afternoon sun is setting, and the cool breeze brushes against my skin.

My sister starts talking about her class; at least her afternoon was more exciting than mine.

When the Torres family adopted me, I was only five years old. I tried to adapt to my new sister until I realized that all she wanted was for me to be myself. She is only a year older than me, and our connection was almost immediate, as if I had been born into this family.

"Helena, what do you think of Lucas?" she asks, pulling me out of my reverie.

"Which Lucas?" I raise an eyebrow, looking at her.

"Which Lucas, seriously, sis? The one from your class!"

"Oh, I don't know, he's boring." I kick a stone on the sidewalk.

"Helena, forget about those Arabs. Your fascination is enviable, you know..."

"What can I do if those boys don't interest me?"

We turn the corner, stop in front of our house, and my sister pushes the gate open with both hands.

"They'll never interest you if you don't give them a chance."

The smell of our mother's cooking fills my nostrils.

Since the door is open, I walk through it while Fernanda throws her backpack on the couch.

"HELLO, MY GIRLS," Mom yells from the kitchen.

Guided by the delicious aroma, I enter the kitchen and see Mrs. Solange wiping her hands on her apron.

"Hi, Mom." I walk over to her and receive a kiss on the forehead.

"How was class?"

"Normal." I don't want to go into detail.

"Helena had another run-in with that Vitória," my sister says as she enters.

"And what was the reason this time?" Mom puts her hands on her hips.

"She likes to provoke me, but I don't care. Seriously, her words don't affect me anymore." I sit down in a chair, leaving my backpack beside me. "What are the chances of meeting an Arab someday?" My voice carries a hint of dreaming.

"All the chances, my daughter. Never stop dreaming," Mrs. Solange says proudly.

"And if you ever stop dreaming, go to Mr. Zé's bakery; there are plenty of dreams there."

I look at Fernanda indignantly as she bursts into laughter, and Mom tries to stifle a smile. I can't hold it in and start laughing along.

CHAPTER ONE

Helena

"Fernanda, please, can't you see I'm trying to record this video?" I look away from the camera and at my sister.

"Helena, this video isn't even going to reach him anyway."

I watch my sister lie down on my bed.

"Hope is the last to die..."

"In your case, it should have died a long time ago."

I roll my eyes.

"Your persistence in my relationship is enviable, Nanda," I murmur.

"I just wish you'd give it up; after all, it's been years of this obsession. You're twenty-two, recently graduated; go enjoy life, sis." She props herself up on her elbows, still lying down and looking at me.

I exhale forcefully.

"I'm going to send just one more video; I need to try one more time..."

"When you told me you got the number of this guy's assistant, I almost thought it would work, but it didn't. We need to admit that this guy, whose name I can't recall, is practically untouchable. If only he were fascinated by someone more modest. But no, it's the sheikh, the owner of all that stuff."

I smile as I see my sister sit up on the bed.

Fernanda has always been very realistic; many times she's made me face reality and realize I might be dreaming too big.

In one of the many searches I did, I managed to get in touch with a Muslim, Kaled. We exchanged a few messages, and that was enough for us to become good friends. Surprisingly, he managed to get Nain Khan Al-Abadi's email, one of Fazza's assistants, the current president of Agu Dhami.

I've been following Fazza's life for a few years. He took over as president when his father passed away, becoming the emir of Agu Dhami. In other words, Fazza has been in charge for three years.

Even if I were in the UAE, I wouldn't be able to get close to him; the man is untouchable.

I don't know how this fascination with Islamic culture started; I believe it was during one of the topics in school when I researched more deeply about it and ended up becoming enchanted. Since then, I've been following everything about the royalty of the seven United Arab Emirates and even learned the language.

I've prepared myself to pursue my dream.

"If I were you, I'd try to get to know this Kaled better." Fernanda pulls me out of my reverie.

"He's just a friend."

"A friend who does everything for you, even got you this email, though I think it's probably deactivated. How many messages have you sent them?"

"I don't know, I've lost count." I shrug, getting up from the chair, noticing my shirt had lifted while I was sitting and pulling it down.

"You're so beautiful, Helena, to be wasting your time on this. There are millions of Brazilians to fall in love with, and I'm talking about real men, not this platonic crush where you don't even know the guy."

I don't reply because I don't want to admit that I've lost and that all these years have been a waste of time.

I raise my arms, gathering my hair into a bun.

I return to the notebook, pause, and save the video. Without realizing I have Nain's email open, I send the video I recorded talking with my sister.

As soon as I realize what I've done, I try to cancel it, but it's in vain.

"Oh no, no, no, no..."

"What's wrong?" Fernanda rushes over to see what happened.

"I sent the video of us talking." Frustrated, I start pacing back and forth.

"Oh, that? Relax! They won't see it anyway. How many videos have you sent and none have been answered?"

I stop pacing and look at my sister.

"Yeah, you're right."

"I'm going to the beach; do you want to come? Matheus said he invited a friend."

Nanda always tries to push her boyfriend's friends on me.

"No, thanks. I need to send out some resumes."

Now that I've finished the course, I want to work in my field. After all, I didn't study economics for four years to end up in a dead-end job.

"Helena, please, let's go. Stop being a killjoy; I'll help you send the resumes later." She pouts, clasping her hands together.

"Alright, fine, you win! Let's go." I force a smile as she claps her hands.

I go to the wardrobe, open the drawer, and grab a bikini.

Living in Rio de Janeiro has its perks, especially when there's a beach nearby to cool off the heat.

Fernanda heads to her room to change, while I get ready.

We're three women living together, so there's no need to go to the bathroom to change when we have our privacy.

Mrs. Solange works as a housekeeper for some rich folks here in Rio. She works hard to support us, and I financed my education through a government loan, so now I need a good job to pay off the installments.

Fernanda got a scholarship, so she did almost her entire course for free. My sister works at a law firm, and her bosses helped her with college.

I tie the bikini straps, look at my reflection in the mirror, and notice my flat stomach from the daily morning workouts before sunrise. I let my hair fall in long wavy cascades, then gather it into a bun on top of my head. I grab a cover-up, tie it around my waist, and walk around the room in light, neutral tones.

I don't have much here, just a double bed, a wardrobe, and a desk where I study.

I head to my notebook, sit in the chair, about to close it when I see the notification for a new email.

I gulp as I see the name on the notification.

Nain responded.

Shit!

I breathe heavily; this must be a bad joke.

I open the email and then let out a scream.

No, no, no, no...

He opened the video.

"What happened, Helena?" Fernanda rushes into the room, horrified.

"He responded," I murmur, stunned.

My sister stops beside me, and we read the first line of the message together:

"Sheikh Fazza Bin Khalifa Ahmad Al-Sabbah requests your presence at the Agu Dhami Palace."

"Damn it, Helena, DAMN IT!" my sister screams beside me, jumping up and down.

CHAPTER TWO

Fazza

"Wait." I hold the tablet in my hand before handing it to Nain. "Whose email is this?" I ask, already opening the notification.

"This person is persistent. I thought I had blocked this email address."

I glance up at my assistant while crossing my leg, seated in the presidential chair.

"There's a video." Curious, I press play and hear Nain sigh.

"Don't we have enough tasks already, Fazza?"

I ignore him.

The image of a beautiful young woman appears on the screen.

"Hello, my name is Helena Simões."

Her voice is soft.

"This might be my last video, since I haven't received any feedback on the last few occasions."

"I don't want to believe all my effort was in vain."

"Mr. Nain, I know you work for the sheikh of Agu Dhami and would like an opportunity to speak with him."

"Bold girl!" Nain says behind me, watching the video along with me.

My eyes fix on her dark brown hair falling in curls over her shoulders, and I wonder if it's silky or soft.

I continue paying attention to what the girl is saying:

"I'm Brazilian, living in Rio de Janeiro, but I'm willing to do anything to come to Agu Dhami."

My eyes light up.

"Sheikh, I don't like your silence."

I raise my hand, scratching my beard.

The video is interrupted when another young woman enters the room, and they start speaking in Portuguese. I understand a bit of the language, and since I don't practice often, I don't remember many words.

But I understand most of what is said in the recording.

Apparently, the other girl's name is Fernanda, and she's lecturing sweet Helena, all because she wants to visit my Emirate.

I want her here!

I want this young woman in my palace.

I hold my breath when I see Helena get up from the chair, showing off a short skirt. I glance back, not realizing I'm being possessive with Nain, to make him turn his face away from the young woman.

By Allah, her stomach is exposed, and I imagine what it would be like to feel her skin against mine.

"I want this young woman here. Arrange it, Nain," I say without thinking as soon as the video ends.

"Sheikh, this woman is not from here. She isn't even Muslim."

"She can convert; that's not a problem." I shrug, standing up. "Reply to the email and send all the details. I want Helena here as soon as possible."

"Fazza, let's be rational. And what about your wives?"

I stop in front of the window and look at the lake in the distance. I close my eyes for a brief moment, and green eyes come to mind.

Who is this young woman, and why does she want to meet me so badly?

"What about my wives?" I ask, not looking at Nain.

"They won't like having a junior wife."

"I want Helena for one specific purpose, Nain," I say, slowly turning my face towards my assistant.

"I'm afraid to ask what that purpose might be."

"I know it goes against our customs, but I want this Brazilian for my pleasure. Zaya only comes to my bed as if it's an obligation. I don't like forcing her to do anything, and even when I make it pleasurable, she acts coldly. Samira is pregnant and cannot come to my room."

Zaya and Samira are constantly at odds, and I wonder why they are this way when I give both of them the same treatment.

After Zaya had our third daughter, Samira discovered she was pregnant, and I was left with only one wife again.

Samira is confident she's expecting my first son, and I pray to Allah every day that this is true.

Sometimes this family tradition of finding out the baby's gender only after birth frustrates me; it's nine months of anxiety, living in uncertainty about whether my son is on the way or not.

"Are you sure a third wife won't make things worse?"

I don't answer his question, but I firmly state what I want:

"Just bring Helena Simões to my palace, and I want her covered. I don't want another sheikh coveting my future wife."

"Are you sure, sir?" Nain picks up the tablet from my desk.

"Yes, I am. I don't go back on something I've already said."

I let my assistant respond to the email and walk towards the door.

"Fazza?"

I turn towards the voice of my brother calling me.

"Is there a problem, Khalil?" I raise an eyebrow, walking beside my brother.

"Did Omar come by?"

"And why should he have come by?" I ask another question on top of his.

"No, never mind. Your mother is looking for him and asked me to check if he was here."

"The years go by, and nothing changes." I huff.

Omar is my brother by both father and mother, while Khalil is only by father. They are the ones I talk to the most, though my and Omar's opinions are somewhat controversial.

I believe Omar still hasn't forgiven Father for choosing me over him, even though he's the eldest son.

"Where is Nain?"

I descend the stairs with my brother and find few men walking around.

"I gave him a task..." I let the sentence trail off.

"I hope it's not something too controversial, brother."

"You'll find out soon enough."

A smile crosses my lips as I recall the features of the sweet Brazilian. Her upturned nose, the well-defined eyebrows on her face, and her slightly plump lips.

What would they taste like?

"Fazza, Fazza..." My brother already senses that I have something on my mind.

Like me, my brothers are considered sheikhs, as we are born of a sheikh lineage.

We inherited the title from the cradle.

"Remember, Fazza, you need to choose the new prince."

I exhale forcefully.

"I'm confident that Samira will give me my first son. Otherwise, I will choose a temporary member to replace me if necessary."

"I pray to Allah every day to grant you your son."

We remain silent as we cross the palace towards the private part, where our residence is located.

CHAPTER THREE

Helena

"No. I'm against you going," Fernanda says, looking at me in terror.

"Stop being ridiculous, what could happen?" I cross my legs, sitting on the sofa.

"He might propose to you, and you, being as crazy as you are, might accept." My sister paces back and forth.

"Don't worry, sis, everything will be fine," I try to reassure her.

"I would love to go with you," Mom says with a kind voice. "But I can't leave my duties."

"Please, sis, use your head. Don't let this man influence you, you don't even know him."

Sometimes my sister treats me as if I were her daughter.

I look at my suitcase ready in the middle of the room and thank myself for having bought a hijab once; it's the only piece of Arab clothing I own.

I get up from the sofa, walk over to each of them, and give a kiss on the cheek along with a tight hug.

"Wish me luck," I say as I grab the handle of my suitcase.

"I'll wish for you to come back, sis, I don't want to lose you." Nanda pouts.

The ride-share car is already waiting for me outside the house.

With one last wave, I leave my home in Rio de Janeiro.

I'm scared of the unknown, but at the same time curious. I know a lot about Arab culture, but nothing I've seen up close.

After a week of talking with Mr. Nain, with his influence, I managed to expedite my visa, and my passport was ready quickly.

I'm leaving Brazil for the first time!

My hands are sweating, and just thinking about the possibility of seeing Fazza Bin Khalifa Ahmad Al-Sabbah in front of me makes my whole body tense.

Will he meet with me?

After all, I am just a single woman.

I DESCEND AT AGU DHAMI airport and am taken aback by the almost infernal heat.

When I boarded the plane to Agu Dhami, I wore my hijab, arriving at my destination appropriately.

Wearing jeans and white sneakers, I feel my legs begging for fresh air.

I pass by people, confused about where to go, following the signs until I spot an Arab holding a sign with my name and go towards him.

The man was serious until he saw me.

"Hello," I whisper as I approach. "I'm Helena Simões."

"Let's go, ma'am. Nain asked me to take you to a shopping center to buy appropriate clothing. After that, you'll stay in a hotel until further notice."

I agree, believing I understood everything that was said since the man spoke too quickly in his native language.

I follow the man who guides me to a black car where my suitcase is stored.

I sit in the back seat of the car.

"What's your name, please?" I ask the man who sits in the passenger seat.

"Habib," is all he says.

The driver wears white attire and constantly looks in the rearview mirror, while Habib fiddles with his phone, distracted.

I take out my phone and send a message to my sister letting her know that I arrived safely. I take a photo through the car window to show her the scenery and complain about the heat here.

The driver slows down and stops in front of a hotel. Soon someone opens my door, and I step out, one foot at a time, and stand at the entrance, observing the building, which is entirely made of glass.

I raise my face to analyze the height, but the sunlight quickly blinds me.

I lower my face again; Habib signals for me to follow him, and I do.

At the reception, he says my name, and I see that the driver takes my bag. I try to grab my luggage, but I'm intercepted.

I'm just a puppet guided by them.

I'm amazed by the beauty of the place; it's all surreal and nothing like anything I've seen in my life.

We stop in front of the elevator door, which soon opens. I lower my face, as I don't want to make eye contact with anyone.

We reach our floor, and the two men accompany me to the entrance of my room. The driver leaves my suitcase and exits silently, while Habib says:

"Change of plans, someone will come to your room to bring appropriate clothing. You'll have a few hours to rest. Afterwards, you'll go to the palace; the emir desires your presence."

"Today?" I ask, astonished.

"Yes, today," the man replies as if I were a child.

Habib hands me the card that unlocks the door and leaves.

I enter the room, pushing the bag inside and look around. A huge bed is in the center of the room in light tones.

The air conditioning is on, making me sigh with relief at the coolness.

I walk to the bed, throw myself onto it, and stare at the ceiling, straining my eyes to observe the plasterwork.

Or is it not plaster?

I don't know.

I take off my hijab, using my feet to remove my sneakers.

Why does the Sheikh want my presence so quickly?

Fazza always looks very serious in photographs, and it's clear from his social media that he doesn't manage it himself. The emir of Agu Dhami doesn't look like someone who procrastinates on social media.

I'm startled when I hear someone knock on the door. I jump up and go to it, opening it.

"Ah!" the woman clears her throat. "May I come in? I have your clothing."

She is fully covered, wearing a hijab with a tunic.

"Come in." I gesture for her to enter. "I'm Helena."

"Nice to meet you, Helena. I'm Isa; I work for the royal family." She smiles, bringing a clothing rack with her.

I help her push it to the center of the room.

"Wow, Isa, why so much stuff?" I ask, amazed.

"Nain asked me to bring everything, as no one knows how many days you'll be staying."

I agree, looking at the colorful clothes on the rack and various scarves.

"Do you know what I can wear today?"

"Nain confided in me that you are a guest of the emir, correct? No one in the palace knows about you. Fazza is very discreet about his decisions, but he likes to see his women well-dressed and hates that they might be seen by other men. There are rumors that he is quite possessive, but we know that all Arabs are, including my husband, Nain."

I smile upon learning that she is Nain's wife, the man I spoke with.

Isa takes a box with a golden jewel, and I widen my eyes at the sight of the necklace and matching dark green earrings, almost the same shade as my eyes.

"Wear this, Helena, the emir ordered."

"I see he doesn't only rule in his Emirate," I murmur, watching the woman smile.

"*I hope you know what you're getting into, sister,*" Fernanda's voice echoes in my mind.

"I'll help you choose a dress that will cover your body and, at the same time, be inviting to the eyes of our sheikh," Isa says with a sparkle in her eyes.

"Inviting? What do you mean?" I ask, raising an eyebrow.

"Wait, you don't know?"

I realize Isa has no filter.

"I don't know what, Isa? If you started, finish it."

"The emir plans to marry you."

"What?" I almost yell.

CHAPTER FOUR

Helena

I rub my hands together as I observe my reflection in the mirror.

The tunic that covers me down to my feet is light green, and the fabric is light and comfortable.

I trace the collar around my neck with the tips of my fingers, and the hijab hides my hair.

Isa's words keep replaying in my mind.

The sheikh wants to marry me?

But doesn't he already have two wives?

I've always been fascinated by the life he leads and all this world of luxury.

But I never considered marrying a sheikh.

Who am I kidding? Of course, I've considered it, and multiple times.

Two knocks on the door are heard, and I go to open it.

"Are you ready, madam?" Habib asks me.

"Yes, just a second, I'll grab my phone."

I walk over to the bed, grab my phone and a handbag to carry my documents and room key card.

I follow Habib.

We leave the busy hotel and find the driver waiting for us.

I sit in the back seat of the car and, as it starts moving, I look at the scenery around me, with several luxurious buildings and not a cloud in the sky.

I want to visit all the tourist spots I researched online; I wonder if I'll get the chance.

Well, if I can't, I'll go anyway.

I drift in my thoughts, and this time it takes a while to arrive.

The car slows down, turns around, and I see the palace in the distance, the monument I've seen so many times online.

Soon the car stops next to other vehicles, and I realize that this place is reserved for those close to the royal family.

I get out of the car as soon as they open my door, look around, and swallow hard. I never imagined the place would be like this, even in my wildest dreams.

"Please follow me," Habib requests.

I follow the man.

We walk through a marble corridor, and I discreetly trace the wall with the tips of my fingers as we go.

Everything is immaculate, white, and clean.

When we stop in front of a door, Habib takes off his shoes, and I mimic the gesture, remembering one of their customs not to bring dirt from the street inside the house.

"Wait here." He points to the room.

It seems to be a waiting area, with two white sofas facing each other and an armchair at one end.

The window is covered with a sheer ice-colored curtain, letting the street light in.

"Would you like something to drink, madam?"

I shake my head; my nervousness prevents me from drinking anything.

Habib leaves the room, leaving me alone. I walk to the window, push the curtain aside, and look through the glass.

There's a courtyard, and a girl is sitting on a stool reading a book. Is she his daughter?

I know he has three daughters with his first wife, but I'm not sure how many people live here.

The girl lifts her face from the book; her hair is loose, and she's wearing a light pink tunic. She looks at me smiling, and I return the gesture without realizing someone has entered the room.

With a clear throat, I turn my face.

I swallow hard as I see the man standing in front of me. I'm definitely not prepared for this moment.

Fazza is wearing a white tunic, his thick black hair is trimmed in a masculine cut, his beard perfectly frames his face, and as in the photos, he's serious and even more handsome.

Damn!

What do I say in the face of his commanding gaze?

His thick eyebrows accentuating his black eyes complete the perfection of his face.

Oh my God, I'm screwed!

"Miss Simões."

My gaze is captured by the man calling me; it must be Nain.

"Please, have a seat."

I agree, somewhat unsteady, reminding myself that I can still walk.

I stop in front of the sofa, sitting at the edge while Fazza sits in the armchair and Nain on the sofa opposite me.

"We spoke by email; I'm Nain."

"Nice to meet you." I try to be friendly, but I don't think I am, as Fazza clears his throat.

I glance at the arrogant man crossing his legs and scratching his beard.

"Emir, do you want me to go over the terms of the contract, or would you prefer to do it yourself?"

"Leave us alone. Wait at the door, and I'll call you if needed."

The man's voice is deep, causing my body to react.

With a nod, Nain leaves the room.

I can't bring myself to look directly at the sheikh. When he doesn't return my gaze, it's easy to observe him, but when he looks at me, it becomes more difficult.

"Helena?"

Hearing my name on his lips is like a melody.

"Look at me."

Without questioning, I look in his direction.

"That's better. How was the trip?"

Is he seriously asking me about the trip?

I raise an eyebrow and reply:

"It was good." I shrug.

"How far are you willing to go to immerse yourself in my culture?" He gets straight to the point, making me swallow hard. "Would you like some tea?"

I shake my head.

"Why did you ask me that?"

Fazza gets up from the armchair, takes a few steps to the sofa where I'm sitting, and sits next to me with minimal distance.

"I want you to be my wife, sweet Helena."

I widen my eyes.

Fazza doesn't beat around the bush; he gets straight to the point, but how do I respond to such a sudden question?

"I... I... I don't know. Honestly, I wasn't expecting this," I murmur.

"I want you, Helena, but it has to be my way and within my culture. I need you to accept and be willing to do everything to be by my side, but with one caveat: I want you to satisfy my desires."

"How?" I say without thinking. "Like as a... a..." It seems the words escaped my mouth.

"No! You will be my wife, but with a contract, in which you will be mine to fulfill my desires. Both parties will benefit, and of course, you will be rewarded."

Fazza must be out of his mind; this man must have hit his head.

I get up from the sofa because I need to distance myself from him; his penetrating gaze makes me feel disoriented. I stop in front of one of the windows and look through the curtain, barely seeing anything on the other side while I remain silent, trying to process what has been said.

Am I willing to give up everything to fulfill a dream?

My body tenses when I feel Fazza behind me.

"You don't need to answer now, but I need you to be quick. I will pay your dowry and a little extra for closing this deal with me, but no one can know about this, especially not your sister and mother."

I turn my body immediately, not realizing how close he is, and lift my face.

Fazza is a few centimeters taller than me.

"How do you know about my mother and sister?" I ask, astonished.

"I know everything about you, Helena Simões. I know you were adopted and where your parents are."

"Ho... how?" I inhale his strong scent, something that stays imprinted in my mind.

I've never encountered a man with such a strong scent.

"Nothing escapes my notice." He examines the features of my face. "I want to take off your hijab, feel the taste of your skin, but I can't, not before we formalize an engagement."

I close my eyes as I feel his hand lift and touch my face.

My body feels like it's about to catch fire.

"I need to think; this is too much," I murmur, opening my eyes to meet his intense black gaze.

"I'll give you until tomorrow to think. I want you back here after the second prayer of the day."

I agree, remembering that they have the habit of performing five prayers a day.

"Remember, I can double the amount. I know you care a lot about your mother and sister, and I can ensure their retirement if you agree to marry me."

"That's a low blow," I say, wanting to touch him.

Fazza lowers his face with his eyes fixed on mine. Unexpectedly, he presses his lips to mine in a brief kiss, so quick that I didn't even get to feel their softness, as if doing it just to test me.

"I need to go now, sweet Helena. Think about my proposal. If you go out in the city, take Habib with you and stay covered. I don't want anyone looking at the future new princess."

I widen my eyes.

He's already taking me as his future wife. When they said he was possessive, they forgot to mention he's also quite controlling.

CHAPTER FIVE

Helena

I **slept** so poorly last night, with doubts haunting me, and to make matters worse, I couldn't talk to my mother or Nanda.

Fazza wants an answer today, but the problem is that I don't have one.

Still lying down, I open my eyes and stare at the ceiling.

What makes me slightly inclined to accept is the fact that I could secure my mother's retirement. I could pay for the years she took such good care of me and let my old lady rest.

I know that Nanda will judge me, call me crazy, but I will accept.

They won't be able to know anything about the pleasure contract.

Oh, heavens!

This man must be crazy. How can I give pleasure to someone if I'm still a virgin?

I know how it all works in theory. Nanda has always told me about her steamy encounters and how bold she is behind closed doors.

But what about me?

In practice, I don't know anything.

Why does Fazza want me?

I'm a virgin, just like the women he has married.

I sit on the bed, not worrying about the time, and get up slowly to head to the bathroom.

I turn on the shower, leave my pajamas on the floor, feel the water to check how pleasant it is, and look through the glass box at the round bathtub.

Will I get used to this new life?

I'll be a princess, the junior wife of the sheikh of Agu Dhami, the greatest of the seven United Arab Emirates.

But the unanswered question: will I need to convert to Islam?

I'm not very devout to Christianity, but I don't intend to convert just like that.

Fazza will have to accept my conditions as well.

I finish my shower, wrap myself in a towel, and head to the clothes rack. I run my hand over the various colors and choose a burnt yellow tunic; the fabric is light and slightly shiny.

I put on my bra and panties, pull the tunic over my head, covering my entire body, and let my hair down from the bun.

The doorbell rings, and I assume it's the coffee.

I rush to the door, open it with a smile on my lips, and am startled to find Fazza standing at my door.

I swallow hard, my eyes wide.

He's wearing a suit instead of his tunic; the shirt has the top two buttons undone, and the sleeves are rolled up to his forearms. The white shirt contrasts nicely with the navy blue pants.

"Fazza?" I finally say.

"I thought we had a meeting."

He sounds irritated, you can tell by the tone of his voice.

"We do, but... but... What the *hell* time is it?"

"You'd better watch your language, Miss Simões," he says, walking past me. "It's one in the afternoon, and you're several hours late."

"Oh, heavens..."

I close the door, watching Fazza walk around the room, observing my mess.

"I see you're not much of a fan of organization," he says in a whisper, entering the bathroom where I just took a shower and left my pajamas on the floor.

"I'll clean up; I didn't realize it was so late. I didn't have a good night's sleep." My voice trails off as he picks up my pajamas from the floor.

I clench my hands as I see him holding the satin fabric between his fingers.

"Do you shower before bed?"

His voice is hoarse, strange...

"Yes..."

Fazza takes my panties from the shorts and puts them in his pocket. *What the hell!*

I squeeze my legs together involuntarily.

"Have you thought about the proposal?" He lifts his face, leaving my pajamas on the floor.

"Why me?" I ask, feeling my leg touch the bed.

"I don't know. Since I saw your video, I wanted you and I still do."

"But don't you already have two wives? Why another one?"

He moves closer.

"Samira and Zaya are very repressed. I've tried everything, but they don't let go in bed. I don't want to seek elsewhere what I don't have, in this case, cheat, so I want a third wife." He stops in front of me, and his perfume fills my senses.

"Fazza, but I'm a virgin," I say bluntly.

"No one has ever touched you, Helena? I mean, intimately?" His eyebrows raise slightly.

"Well, sort of." I let a smile slip from my lips, seeing him snort.

"What do you mean, sort of? Has any man ever touched you? Tell me where you've been touched."

My cheeks heat up; I'm not going to tell him that...

Oh, but I really won't!

"Sorry, I don't know if this is on the table here." I try to move away from him, but I feel his hand grip my arm.

"I'm talking to you, Helena."

His voice is somewhat serious, making me tremble internally.

I turn my face to look over my shoulder.

"Don't you have two wives? I didn't ask you what you do with them, so I won't tell you about me."

Fazza narrows his eyes.

"Allah, Allah... These are two opposite situations."

"Without a doubt." I am sarcastic. "Moreover, I'm not sure if I can handle this polygamy thing. I don't know if I'll be able to stand other women touching my husband."

Fazza pulls my arm, making me stop in front of him, and I release my breath with difficulty due to my imbalance.

"That's not an obstacle; we can resolve that later..." He shrugs.

"All this so I sign this contract? And if I don't sign?"

Fazza takes a strand of my hair between his fingers, and I watch him twirl it around his fingers.

"If you don't sign, I'll try to persuade you." He fixes his eyes on mine.

"I need to know all the clauses of this contract, and there's another thing: I don't want to convert."

Fazza huffs.

"Before you say anything, I'll be present at all the rituals; I might even consider the possibility, but I'm not ready to abandon my customs. While we're here, I'll wear all the clothing according to your wishes, but when we leave this country..."

Fazza releases my hair, and I look at his thick beard, very close.

"Alright, after all, I don't want to have children with you. Our purpose will always be different."

I admit his words hit me hard, but I remain strong.

"I'll have our marriage contract prepared. Are you okay with that, Helena?" His hand moves to my face and caresses it.

"Yes, you can have it prepared. But know that I'll read it first."

He lets a smile slip.

"Alright, when it's ready, Nain will contact you. I need to go now."

I close my eyes as I realize he lowers his face to mine. He presses his lips to mine, this time a lingering kiss, long enough to let out a sigh through my mouth.

"I want you, Helena, and I will have you in my bed," he says with his face close, his nose brushing mine, and the scent imprinted in my mind.

Fazza steps back and winks before leaving the room.

I let my body fall onto the bed, sitting there, waiting for the mix of emotions to pass.

One thing is clear: Fazza is fighting for his customs in a nearly lost battle between desire and his duty as an emir.

CHAPTER SIX

Fazza

I **observe** Samira sitting on the sofa and my mother next to her. They are chatting animatedly.

I make some noise entering, drawing their attention.

"Fazza, dear." My mother lifts her gaze with a smile on her lips.

"Where is Zaya?" I ask about my first wife.

"She must be in the bedroom with the little one."

"Have her called," I order one of the maids. "Omar, Khalil, stay; what I have to say is brief and there's no need for delays."

I sit in the central armchair in the living room and assess Samira's curves. With her belly being this size, she must be halfway through her pregnancy.

My marriage to Samira was an arrangement I made with her father, a Greek. She is Greek and converted to Islam without question.

Since she arrived in this house, she's stuck to my mother like a tick, and I don't mind, as long as she is happy, I know I will have a lasting marriage.

As for Zaya, it's always been more complicated. I married her because I thought I loved her, but after the marriage, she became frigid and only comes to my bed out of obligation.

I notice Zaya entering the room with our eldest daughter, Safira, who is seven years old.

When everyone is in the room, my daughter looks at me with her bright little eyes, and I offer her my best smile.

Even though I don't have a son yet, I love each of my three daughters with Zaya.

"Taking advantage of the fact that everyone is here, I am informing you, without question, as the decision has already been made, that I have a girlfriend who will eventually become my junior wife."

"What?" Omar is the first to speak, almost shouting.

Samira sniffs, trying to hold back her tears.

"Son, could you have a bit of pity for your pregnant wife with our first male child?" Mom hugs Samira.

"Well, I'm eager to meet your girlfriend," Zaya says in a tone for everyone to hear.

I narrow my eyes at her; my first wife has average beauty and is straightforward in all her statements.

"Thank you, Zaya. As I said, there's no reason to question; my decision has been made."

"And who is she? Why, my sheikh, why?" Samira asks through her tears.

Her crying must be due to the fear of losing her novelty status in the house. Once, she asked me not to take a third wife, and of course, I didn't answer, since one never knows what tomorrow will bring.

Samira is ambitious; she wants all the attention on her, and with Helena around, she might not get that.

When we were dating, Samira seemed sweet, but after marriage, she showed her true colors. She even asked to be my only wife, which of course, did not happen.

"Her name is Helena, a Brazilian."

"Oh no, this must be a joke! A Westerner, Fazza?" Mom starts pacing back and forth.

"Yes, mother, a Westerner. Any other questions?"

"Where did you meet this woman?" Samira asks amidst her sighs.

"That's not relevant." I rise from the armchair. "I think that's all; my day is long." I leave the room with Nain and Khalil following me.

I slip on my sandal as I pass through the door, and the hot air of Agu Dhami hits my body, which is why I prefer wearing a tunic; it's cooler in the heat.

"Brother, a third wife, what madness," Khalil says as we pass through the corridor.

"Not you too, Khalil," I murmur in disgust.

"I'm happy for you, brother," Khalil finally says.

I glance sideways at Nain; no one can know about the pleasure contract I made with Helena. After all, marriage is meant for having children, and in my case, I don't want her for that purpose.

I want Helena to be mine; I desire this woman in every way since the first moment I saw her in that video.

And in person, she's even more beautiful.

I'm eager to see her without that tunic, naked for me. I want to feel her skin and hold every part of her body.

Yesterday, I felt her hair; it's so soft, silky, and fragrant.

I know everything about her life; it wasn't too hard to find out, and when I mentioned that I knew who her real parents were, surprisingly, she didn't even pay attention.

Does she know who they are, or does she truly not care?

After all, she was abandoned at an orphanage and adopted at five by this Brazilian family.

Helena has a degree in economics, and that might be a problem. Western women tend to meddle in men's affairs, and I hope she stays away from that.

"Emir," Nain says, breaking my reverie. "The President of the United States would like to schedule a conference with you. He requested it urgently."

I grunt; our alliance with the Americans sometimes causes a tremendous headache.

"You can fit it into my schedule. Ask Helena to come to my office; we need to finalize the details," I murmur without providing information in front of my brother.

"I'm going to the mosque; I need to discuss some matters with Mohammad," my brother announces before leaving.

"Sir, when do you plan to announce your new marriage?" Nain inquires in a whisper.

"As soon as Helena signs the contract. Once she does, we will be certain that the commitment is sealed. Until then, we can tell everyone that we are dating until the day of our wedding."

Nain nods.

While we are dating, I will have time to get to know her better, although what I really want is to get to know her intimately.

I admit I was a bit bothered when she didn't agree to convert, but since I want her only for my pleasure, I don't mind, *not for now,* since we won't be having children, so there's no problem with this issue.

CHAPTER SEVEN

Helena

"**HELENA SIMÕES**" Fernanda practically shouts from the other end of the line. "I can't believe you accepted this crap!"

I move the phone slightly away from my ear while I look at the scenery through the car window.

"I knew you'd react like this, but I'm fine. He's going to pay my dowry, and I'll send it to mom, so I can ensure a better future for her and still pay off my college debt," I say, listening to her huff.

"Of course, it's not an excuse, sister. Think carefully if this is really what you want. Your happiness is at stake, and if you tell me this is what you want, I'll be by your side, supporting your decisions. If you ever want to run away from this man, I'll help you." Nanda's voice is choked up. "I can't believe my little sister is getting married and I won't be there."

We smile.

"I really wanted you and mom here," I murmur melancholically.

"Please, Helena, don't let this man mold you. Don't let him take away your wonderful essence. And keep sending me photos; I want to feel like I'm there with you."

We remain silent, each listening to the other's breathing.

Fernanda has always been my best friend, confidant, and sister, and hiding the main fact of this marriage from one of the most important people in my life breaks my heart.

We end the call, both of us emotional.

I wipe a tear from my face as the car pulls up near the palace. This time, we enter through the main entrance.

Beside me is Habib, guiding me in silence.

I adjust my hijab with my hair hidden underneath the fabric as I notice some tourists looking in my direction. After all, I'm wearing one of the jewels that Fazza sent me.

I once read in a newspaper that the palace is made of Italian marble. Everything here is so lavish and beautiful.

Habib glances back when he notices I'm distracted by the surroundings. I don't think I'll ever get used to this.

I quicken my pace, catching up with Habib as we enter the palace. I'm led through several corridors, mostly in light colors, whites, and golds. I'm almost inclined to say that the gold is real gold.

Habib stops in front of a door, knocks twice, and a voice grants us entry.

I enter what appears to be an office, and Fazza is behind a desk, looking at a laptop.

His gaze soon lifts to my direction.

"Sit down, Helena."

My bare feet feel the softness of the carpet in the room.

I sit on the sofa in the corner of the room and look at the books on the shelf, all with titles in Arabic and English.

Fazza stands up, and I see that his tunic fits him very well. On his head, there's a *Ghtrah* white, draping over his shoulder and covering his hair.

The sheikh dismisses the men present, leaving him alone with me.

I feel my body tense, and I don't know why I feel this way in his presence.

"How was your two days away from me?" he asks, sitting beside me.

"Well, I visited many places with Isa's help."

Isa has proven to be a good friend; she's friendly and loves to talk.

"I believe it." He hands me some papers. "Here is the contract. If you agree with everything, we will announce our relationship and then proceed with the wedding."

I forgot that dating here is different from the Brazilian way. Technically, dating is for the couple to get to know each other better and marry if they feel compatible.

Which is not our case; after all, dating is just a pretext for the wedding day.

"Is there already a deadline for our wedding?" I ask, reading between the lines.

"As soon as possible..."

"And that would be in how many days or months?" I lift my eyes from the papers, looking at the sheikh.

"At the latest, two months."

I agree.

Two months...

Okay, two months to become the princess of the sheikh of Agu Dhami.

I lower my face again, unable to focus on what's written, not with Fazza beside me.

"Am I interrupting?"

It seems he noticed my distraction.

"Your presence sometimes intimidates me," I say, lifting my face towards him.

His features are serious and harsh, and his mouth is slightly pink in a natural tone.

"Why would I do that?" he asks, raising his hand.

He runs his fingers over my hijab, removing the fabric from my head.

Hypnotized by his touch, I notice the moment he releases my hair, letting the curls fall to my shoulders.

"Why do I intimidate you, Helena?" he asks again with a serious and slightly husky voice.

"I don't know, everything about you screams lust, and that's new to me."

"Why did you send those emails if you're afraid of me?"

I bite the corner of my lip when I see him do the same.

"I'm not afraid, I just feel like a little bird near a cat, about to be devoured." I place the papers beside me.

Without him saying anything, I act on impulse, in the heat of the moment, wanting more of his touch.

I lift my tunic slightly, sitting on his lap, positioning my legs around his waist.

Fazza is taken by surprise but doesn't remove me from his lap. On the contrary, his hands reach for my leg and move up my thigh.

His touch leaves trails of heat wherever he goes.

"Helena, what do you want?" he asks with a husky voice.

"I want you," I murmur, holding his neck with the tips of my fingers, feeling the soft beard.

Without asking for permission, I press my lips to his. I don't want a peck; I want more.

I want to feel his tongue in my mouth and his caresses.

The kiss starts as a peck but quickly deepens. His tongue demands entry, and I allow it. My face arches slightly, demanding more of the kiss while one of his hands grabs my hair, holding it tightly, making me moan.

I have never felt so at someone's mercy as I do now.

I press our bodies closer, rubbing my intimacy against his member, which starts to make its presence known.

My hand travels down his arm, feeling his muscles, and I release another sigh when he nibbles on my lip.

Suddenly, he stops, tossing me to the side of the sofa, standing up, and stepping away.

"This can't happen again. Not before the wedding. This is betrayal, Helena!"

His voice is hoarse, and he doesn't look in my direction, making me feel like a creature.

I don't say anything, feeling my breath coming in ragged gasps.

"Put on your hijab. We won't be alone from now on; you are even more tempting than I thought," he says as if I were an object.

I huff, putting on the hijab haphazardly, just to get out of there.

"I'll read the contract at the hotel and send it back to you signed. Your wish is my command, Your Highness." I make a brief, exaggerated bow in my tone of voice.

Fazza turns towards me.

"I'm going to make things easier for you and stay away."

"You're misunderstanding, Helena, I don't want you to stay away; I just can't control myself when you're near."

I huff like a spoiled child when their present is stolen.

I'm frustrated that he stopped because now that I've tasted his lips, I want more.

"Alright, Fazza, I need to go." I grab the papers and leave the room, stomping my feet.

CHAPTER EIGHT

Fazza

It's been a month since Helena signed the contract, and the palace is in chaos after I announced my wedding.

Not to mention that I've been avoiding Helena.

I can't control myself when I'm near her; it's like I need to have my hands on her body, an urgent need.

I cross my legs watching Zaya, Safira, and Layla dancing in the middle of the room to the music.

I love watching them dance and wonder if Helena knows how to dance like that.

I scratch my beard, imagining the scene.

"When do you plan to bring your girlfriend here, Fazza?" Omar breaks the silence, speaking over the music.

I don't turn my face in his direction; I just watch him from the corner of my eye.

"Tomorrow, I'll announce the date of our wedding."

The room falls into complete silence, except for the music playing while Zaya, Safira, and Layla, my middle daughter, dance.

They still believe that I might back out of this plan, but that's not going to happen. Not until I've satisfied all my desire for Helena.

I'm aware it might be a serious mistake to bring her into my world, given her different culture, and what I fear most is her not handling the fact that I have more than one woman.

She even said she doesn't know if she can handle sharing.

Our relationship has been announced in all the newspapers, and now all eyes are on the new future princess, especially since she is a woman from the West.

"Come on, Dad." Layla extends her tiny hand to dance with me.

I get up, taking my four-year-old daughter's little hand, and dance with my women.

Sometimes I forget how light the situation can be in some moments.

I JERK AWAKE, MY BODY sweaty and a nightmare haunting me.

It's always the same, the same dream comes to mind, the day my father discovered the illness and two days later passed away.

Everything happened so quickly that we didn't get to say a proper goodbye.

Not to mention Omar wanting to steal the throne, being the older brother. He believes he has the right to demand something from me, but not when Dad left everything in my hands and I was the prince trained to lead Agu Dhami.

He asked to appoint his son as the future prince, but I haven't decided yet, and when I feel that the person is right for the position, I will choose.

I sit on the bed; it's still dark. I get up, head to the bathroom, and remove my pajamas, leaving them on the floor. I turn on the shower to wash away the impure sweat from my body and cleanse this nightmare from my soul.

I lather up and Helena comes to mind, the woman who lately hasn't left my thoughts. Especially after I had too many samples of her body, her sweet and inviting lips, her smooth and soft skin.

She responded so well to my touch...

By *Allah*, I was going to have her that day in the office.

I wanted to, I needed to, but I stopped because it was necessary.

I can't let myself be consumed by the pleasures of my body, and as much as I desire Helena, I need to do it in my own way.

I turn off the shower and wrap myself in a towel. I leave the bathroom, go into the closet, and grab a robe.

I need to go to the mosque; perhaps praying will clear these thoughts from my mind.

I open the underwear drawer and find the fabric that has been tormenting me every day.

Why did I take a pair of her panties that day?

Why keep tormenting myself?

I feel the lace with my fingers, squeeze it in my hand, bring it to my nose, and smell it as if it were the most addictive drug.

Shit!

I've always been a rational man, but Helena is throwing me off balance.

I can't act like a lovesick teenager; I'm the emir of Agu Dhami and have an Emirate to care for.

I smell her panties and can taste her cunt. Just imagining that this fabric covered her intimacy, the same intimacy I want to deflower, drives me insane.

With great effort, I put her underwear back away.

"GENTLEMEN, MISS HELENA Simões has arrived."

I'm sitting in my armchair and cross my legs as I see my sweet girlfriend walk through the door.

My family is silent as if they are analyzing and judging her by her appearance.

"It's a pleasure to finally meet you," Zaya says as she stands up. "I'm Sheikha Zaya Ahmad Al-Sabbah, the emir's first wife, but you can call me Zaya."

My first wife approaches Helena and gives her a hug.

I admit I'm surprised by Zaya's warmth. It wasn't like this with Samira; they didn't hit it off right away, and it's clear that they merely tolerate each other.

My mother stands up.

"I'm Sheikha Aiyra Ahmad Al-Sabbah." She walks over to Helena and gives her a quick, noticeably cold hug. "This is Princess Samira, the emir's second wife, and she's expecting his first male heir."

Of course, my mother takes pride in saying this.

The elder said that my male heir would come from my junior wife, and we're all confident that it will be Samira, as she is my junior wife, up to this point.

Soon everyone makes their introductions.

Helena sits next to my eldest daughter, as if they had known each other before, an almost immediate bond.

My eyes don't leave her as she wears a *Khimar* on her head, which is almost like a hijab, the only difference being that it covers more of her face, with the fabric extending over her shoulder.

I get lost in the pink of her lips, the same ones I've kissed and tasted with lust.

Her outfit is baby blue, with some gemstones sparkling on her tunic, and she's wearing the jewel I gave her last time.

Why isn't she wearing the one I sent this morning?

Helena doesn't look in my direction; it's as if she's avoiding me.

But why is she doing that?

I don't understand the reason for her coldness towards me.

CHAPTER NINE

Helena

I **confess** that I am nervous, my muscles are tense, and I'm terrified of laughing at the wrong moment.

Safira is beside me showing off her pearl collection; the girl is smart and knows everything about the subject.

Mrs. Aiyra was somewhat rude, being very direct and implying that she is more in favor of the sheikh's second wife.

I hope the baby is a boy; otherwise, the walls of this palace will shake, since everyone is convinced that it's the sheikh's male heir.

Zaya, the first wife, was friendly and almost thanked me for agreeing to be the emir's wife.

I thought women were like lions with their husbands, but with Zaya, it was the opposite.

Samira didn't stand up to greet me, and it's clear from her look that the second wife doesn't want me here.

I don't want to look in Fazza's direction; I'm somewhat resentful towards him for abandoning me. I've spent this month alone, except for Isa, who visited me often.

I don't even have his phone number and I'm here today because they sent for me.

I thought Arab relationships involved spending more time together to get to know each other better, but that wasn't my case.

After my outburst, where I practically threw myself at him, Fazza disappeared as if I were a contagious disease.

"If you'll excuse me, I'm feeling unwell," Samira says as she stands up with Aiyra's help.

Her belly is moderate and shows little under her tunic.

"Could you accompany me, Fazza?"

She calls him by his first name, and it's the first sign that something inside me isn't ready for the situation. I feel a pang urging me to leave while there's still time, that I'm not prepared to share my husband with other women.

Fazza stands up, placing his hand on Samira's back, and I don't look at the scene; I prefer to keep my head down.

Can I go now?

I've already met all his family.

"As you've just seen, my daughter-in-law is pregnant, and I hope you stay away from her. Samira's pregnancy is very important for this Emirate," Aiyra says as soon as the son leaves the room.

No one says anything.

I lift my face, standing up from the sofa and positioning myself in front of the lady.

"Rest assured, madam, my intention is not to marry her, but him." With a brief nod, I add, "Now if you'll excuse me."

"Where do you think you're going?" the woman scolds me as I turn my back to her.

I don't know how things are done in their culture, but my mother taught me not to be disrespectful and to endure in silence.

I walk along the edge of the room, through a corridor until I find a door leading to the back. The courtyard is vast, with a lion at the center spouting water from its mouth in a beautiful, gleaming fountain, and I walk toward it.

Is this made of gold?

I lower my hand, touching the cool water, and wonder how it can be this temperature on a hot day like today.

I dip my fingers in the water, feeling the refreshing sensation as it passes over my skin.

Do I really want this?

My name is all over the world's newspapers, the new future princess of Agu Dhami.

Sheikh Fazza is marrying a Brazilian for the third time.

The dream of any woman is to be by the side of one of the most powerful men, possibly the most powerful man in the world.

But do I want this?

Will I have the stomach to share my husband?

"Hi."

I lift my face to see a girl crouching beside me.

"I'm Layla, the middle daughter."

I smile at the way the little girl introduces herself.

"Hi, Layla, it's a pleasure. You're very beautiful, you know?"

Layla crouches down and plays with the water alongside me.

"Are you going to marry my father?" the curious girl asks.

"Probably..."

"You won't be boring like Samira, will you?" Layla inquires, fiddling with the water distractedly as she speaks to me.

"I don't think so."

Layla looks at me with her dark eyes, just like her father's.

I smile at her, splashing drops of water on her face, letting out a laugh when I see the girl let out a sly giggle.

The girl doesn't hold back and splashes more water on me, soaking me completely.

I widen my eyes, unable to contain my laughter, and I need to get up when I see her preparing to throw more water.

"Oh, no..." I say amidst my laughter.

Layla leans over, laughing, her hair falling over her shoulder as she writhes with laughter.

"Layla!"

A booming male voice calls for the girl.

We look towards Fazza, who is coming toward us with a serious expression, and beside him is Zaya.

"Dad..." the girl says quietly, scared.

"What is this about?" he inquires rudely to the girl.

"Dad, we were just playing..."

"And is this how a girl behaves?"

He doesn't even let her speak.

"Fazza..." Zaya tries to call her husband, but he doesn't listen.

"You're grounded, Layla!"

"She wasn't at fault." I walk over to the little girl, who is dry compared to me. "I started it, she's just a child and didn't realize how much she could soak me." My voice is assertive, protecting the girl.

Fazza looks at me with a piercing gaze for standing up to him.

"Zaya, take Layla away," he orders.

Zaya practically runs to get her daughter, not before whispering a "thank you."

I am left alone with Fazza, who walks toward me.

"Go back to your hotel room; I don't want to see you in front of me today," he says angrily.

"Fine, you read my mind, because I don't want to see you either. After all, I don't even know why I'm here." I brush past him, deliberately bumping into his shoulder.

I huff, walking quickly, wanting to leave this damned palace and go anywhere away from the sheikh.

I enter a corridor and don't know where I am.

All I want is to get lost in this place!

The corridors are all the same, in white with gold.

I open a door, finding an empty room, and tired of walking, I decide to enter. I quickly remove the headscarf, tossing it on the bed as I let my hair down.

The tunic clings to my body.

Damn it!

I pull the tunic over my head, ending up in just my underwear, and spread the tunic on the bed.

The place looks like a guest room; I think I'll get some peace here.

I'm startled when I see the door open and quickly pull the tunic to cover the front of my body.

"I thought I told you to leave," Fazza says calmly as he sees me without clothes.

"I couldn't find the way out and decided to wait here." I look around as he closes the door behind him, leaving us alone in the room.

"And do you think the exit will appear like magic?"

"Oh, spare me!" I turn my back to him, forgetting that I'm only in my underwear.

"Get dressed, Helena," he murmurs with a hoarse voice.

"You better look now, because I'm not marrying you anymore." I turn to face him. "This body here, you won't have anymore!"

Fazza gives a smile I don't like, so I swallow hard.

"Too late, Helena. You signed the contract, and technically you're already mine. If you break the contract, you'll have to pay me a million dollars."

"Wh... What?" My voice barely comes out.

"Didn't you read the fine print? You're mine, Helena Simões, even against your will."

CHAPTER TEN

Helena

"Tell your emir that I'm feeling unwell." I hang up the phone and throw it on the bed.

I grab the nail polish and paint my toenails.

Fazza had Nain call me to set up a dinner with him, but now I'm the one who doesn't want his presence.

If he thinks he's going to have Helena Simões served on a silver platter, he's sorely mistaken. I'll give him the pleasure of the challenge.

Even though I desire the man, he needs to understand that I'm not like his submissive wives.

I brush the polish on the last nail and lift my foot against the wall.

Bored, I stare at the ceiling.

I came back from the street so angry at Fazza that I took a shower and have been in just my underwear ever since.

How could I have been so foolish?

I practically sold myself to this man; I must have shit in my head.

I let myself be swept away, thinking I was in a fairy tale, and in the end, it wasn't like that at all. It wasn't even midnight, and the story ended.

I close my eyes, and my phone starts vibrating. I fumble around the bed, grab the device, and see a video call from my sister.

She doesn't know anything about the contract, and I prefer it that way; it's better for her to think the marriage is for love and my future husband wants to see me every day.

I answer the call and see the beach.

"How cruel, huh?" I say, holding the phone above my head.

"You still have time to come back."

I wish, I think ironically.

"You know I'm determined. How are things over there?"

"The same. Boredom has taken over now that I have no one else to annoy." Nanda turns to say something to her boyfriend.

"Nanda, how is Mom?" I ask, trying to get her attention.

"She's fine; every day she complains that you left her. By the way, when are we going to meet your future husband? Is he so busy that he doesn't have a second to talk to his family?" my sister scolds.

"You know it's complicated."

She says nothing.

I frown when I see my sister looking over my shoulder.

"Nena, is that your fiancé behind you? Don't they wear those dreadful dresses?"

"What?" I say, looking back.

Fazza? How did he get in here?

In addition to being intrusive, he manages to be quieter than I expected.

"I'm going to hang up, Nanda..."

"Oh, no, Helena."

Before she can say anything, I hang up the phone.

"I see you have a tendency to be undressed." He points to my lack of clothing.

"I'm not sure if you know the word privacy." I get up from the bed, passing by him and intentionally brushing my shoulder against him.

"What are you going to do?"

"Lock myself in the bathroom. I don't want to see you."

I know I'm being childish, but he's been silent for a damn month.

Before I take another step, Fazza grabs my arm.

"Why are you acting this way?"

I turn my face towards him.

"Seriously, Fazza?" I let out a forced laugh. "You were gone for a month, didn't send me a single 'hi' or speak to me directly. And now you expect me to greet you with a sincere smile? Oh, excuse me, don't expect that, because you won't get it!"

He raises an eyebrow as if he's contemplating the situation.

I try to pull my arm away, but he doesn't let go.

"It was a very hectic month, and I didn't have time for practically anything."

"Great, that explains it." I'm being sarcastic. "I don't believe it."

Fazza's eyes travel down my torso, lingering too long on my breasts, which rise and fall with my rapid breathing.

"I don't need to account for my life to you."

"Then we're even." I confront him.

Maybe acting this way will make Fazza reconsider the contract.

"No, we're not!" His voice is deep.

"So tell me, were you in your wife's bed? Were you with Zaya?"

I know he wouldn't visit Samira because she's pregnant.

Fazza doesn't answer; he doesn't need to. His silence is the answer to my question.

"You ran away from me, but now you're after her." I pull my hand away forcefully, feeling my eyes burn with anger.

"You know it's different; she's my wife."

"To hell with it, Fazza!" I'm trying to control my anger. "We're getting married, and I don't even have your phone number. I can't talk to you before talking to your assistant." I turn my back, wanting to escape.

When I'm almost entering the bathroom, I feel his arms grab me and press me against the wall.

Fazza turns me towards him like a doll, and his body covers mine.

"You know you could have asked me for these damn things." His face is close to mine.

"No, I didn't know. I never know how I should behave in front of you."

"Want my number? I'll give it to you. What else do you want? My attention? I'm here. I'm all yours."

His deep voice saturates my ear, and I close my eyes.

I don't want it, not like this, not as an obligation.

"Aren't you going to say anything?"

I feel his hand on my stomach; his fingers are soft and make my skin burn.

"Where's your courage, Helena? Wasn't this what you wanted?"

His hand moves down, touching my intimacy over my underwear, and I can hear a sigh escape his mouth.

"Is this what you wanted? Wanted to see me break my rules? Don't you understand that it's hard for me?"

I open my eyes, finding his intense black orbs staring at me.

"I don't want this, Fazza. Stop. Don't make me angry with you," I murmur, watching him step back without a flinch and my body feels the emptiness left by him.

I enter the bathroom, grab a robe, wrap myself in it, and tie it tightly.

I return to the bedroom and see Fazza standing by the window. His hands are in his pockets, his expression distant, and his demeanor commanding as if he owns the world.

His face turns to the side, and his expression becomes softer.

"I'm sorry for not keeping in touch. I was an idiot. I thought that staying away would keep me from temptation, but I forgot the most important thing: you."

"Know that I'm a woman of flesh, blood, and feelings; don't treat me just as your pleasure toy."

Fazza walks towards me, his masculine scent filling the room, and his shirt is open at the first few buttons. I focus on his chest with the few visible hairs.

He opens his arms, pulling me to his chest, and I feel his nose in my hair.

With my face pressed against his chest, I sigh, intoxicated by his wonderful scent.

"I can't wait to have you as my wife, Helena..." His voice is a whisper, almost inaudible.

"Is that dinner invitation still on? I'm starving." I lift my head, finding his face close to mine.

"Can we order something here and spend some time together before I go? His lips descend to meet mine, touching in a brief kiss.

"I like the idea." I smile, closing my eyes briefly.

CHAPTER ELEVEN

Helena

We finally got married.
My feet are aching after three days of celebrations, so I'm off to the side, looking around at everything.

My husband has a serene expression, perhaps even excited.

I never thought I'd get married so far from my family. Fazza tried to invite my sister and mother, but they were adamant about not leaving their jobs to come.

I don't blame them; after all, life in Brazil must go on.

My mother-in-law has stayed by my side out of courtesy, but it's clear from her gaze that she doesn't want me here.

I don't know anyone here, except for Isa, who has proven to be a great friend.

Over the past month, Fazza has been very attentive, oddly responding to all my messages even though he didn't appear much, saying it was too difficult to be near me and not be able to touch me.

He takes, or at least tries to take, his culture very seriously.

"May I ask what the bride is doing here alone?" Isa says, pulling me out of my reverie.

"I'm just tired, thinking about when I can leave here," I murmur near her ear.

"I can imagine. I felt the same at my wedding, but then..." She lets the sentence trail off.

I look at my friend's face, which has a slight blush.

"Then what?" I ask, curious.

"Then comes the wedding night. And you know, right? Western women understand more about it."

"Isa, I'm a virgin and don't understand anything in practice," I murmur in her ear, afraid someone might overhear.

"Really? I thought you knew!"

Her face shows amazement, making me roll my eyes.

"Can I ask you a question?" I ask sincerely, and when she nods, I continue, "How was your first time? Did it hurt?"

"Helena!" She scolds me.

"Please, tell me." I clasp my hands, listening to the clinking of the bracelets on my wrist.

She looks at me for a while before finally saying:

"It hurt a little, but Nain was understanding and made it pleasurable for both of us."

I see her cheeks flush again and can't help but smile.

"I'm so scared. I don't even know what I'm doing here; everything seems so confusing."

I know I can confide in Isa; she has proven to be trustworthy many times.

"Everything will be fine. You love each other, and that's what matters."

I just smile.

Little does she know that love is the least involved here.

"Now come on." She takes my hand.

We pass by some people who look at me, and I can't tell if they're analyzing me or admiring me. After all, the second dress of the day contrasts with the numerous jewels that Fazza insisted I wear.

I'm looking around when I meet my husband's intense black eyes.

It's so strange to say, my husband...

I'm married, and everything feels surreal.

He is an emir, considered the king of Agu Dhami, a powerful man, and I am his princess.

It feels like I'm living a dream, and I'm afraid to wake up.

Everything around Fazza is luxurious. He grew up in this world and always knew the amount of millions in his account, unlike me, who preferred not to even check my bank statement for fear of what I might find.

I notice my husband is coming towards me, so I stop walking, waiting for him to arrive while Isa steps aside.

I feel his presence beside me.

I'm afraid I'll end up falling in love and, as a result, getting hurt.

I know the burden he carries, that his customs don't match mine, and that every time I see him with one of his two wives, I'll be jealous.

"Are you tired?" he says near my ear, sending a shiver down my spine.

"Yes." My voice is almost an inaudible whisper, making me nod my head.

"You're finally my wife."

I can feel him breaking into a smile.

Fazza holds both of my hands in a discreet gesture, and his fingers circle around my ring.

"I can't wait to remove your veil and have your hair in my hands." His eyes shine.

If it were possible, I would melt right now; Fazza knows how to destabilize me.

"Fazza..." I murmur.

I'm almost ready to throw myself at his feet when his brother, Khalil, pulls him away. They laugh and move away from me.

I know little about his brothers, but it seems that Khalil is one of his favorites.

I watch the two of them dance.

The party is loud; everyone is laughing and celebrating the emir's new bride, but what everyone forgets is that I'm the bride and I'm right here.

"It looks like you finally made it."

I'm startled when I hear Aiyra speak near my ear.

I look towards my mother-in-law.

"Excuse me?" I raise a confused eyebrow.

"All you foreign women want is a wealthy man. Why not a sheikh? My son has enough money to support even your tenth generation."

I'm shocked at what the woman says.

"To me, he only has one suitable wife, and it's not you." She gives a forced smile and walks away.

I watch my mother-in-law walk away.

It was only a matter of time before she showed her claws.

It's no surprise that she prefers the second wife, especially now that everyone is confident that the baby Samira is carrying is a boy. The longed-for boy that Fazza wants and that all of Agu Dhami Emirate desires.

I huff at such foolishness.

Now, in addition to being tired, I'm irritated and anticipating some very pleasant days with my mother-in-law.

Fortunately, Zaya seems to be a more relaxed person, and there's something strange about her.

But that's neither here nor there.

I can't help but smile when I see my husband dancing. His white tunic with golden accessories gleams, the *Ghtrah* on his head covers his hair, and his well-trimmed beard frames his face perfectly. His jawline is defined, and his thick eyebrows are perfect against his profile.

Fazza is literally a handsome man, at least in my eyes.

I never tire of looking at him, all his elegance, the way he walks upright, how he interacts with the people around him, and still manages to be spontaneous, dancing and engaging with everyone.

I can't fall in love with him, I can't!
Even though it might be too late.

CHAPTER TWELVE

Helena

I feel Fazza's hand slide around my waist as soon as we enter his room.

"Where am I going to sleep?" I ask, seeing the room in the dim light.

"I have a wing in the south of the palace. Zaya and Samira have rooms there, and you will have one as well."

I hold back a sigh.

I can't see the room clearly because he hasn't turned on the light, and only the moonlight coming through the window provides some illumination.

The door to the room closes behind us, and Fazza runs his hand behind my head, releasing the clips from my hair and removing the fabric that covers it, leaving it on some piece of furniture.

I turn my body to face him.

"A bath?"

I raise an eyebrow at the request.

"Now?"

"Yes, this way we leave all our impurities outside. I want you clean and pure."

I always forget these cultural details.

I turn my back to Fazza, signaling for him to unzip my dress.

My husband unzips it, and his finger brushes against my skin.

"I had the bathtub prepared." He moves my hair to the side, kissing my shoulder as my dress falls to the floor.

I'm left in just my panties and bra under my husband's watchful gaze. I remove my bra, then lower my panties, and see that his eyes are clouded.

I turn away, heading towards the open door with a dim light.

I hear the sound of Fazza's clothes falling to the floor, but I don't pay attention. I enter the bathroom with its warm yellow light, look around, and see the bathtub bubbling with a wonderful essence.

I lift my head, observing the intricately worked golden ceiling.

Taking slow steps, I stop in front of the bathtub, touch the warm water with the tips of my fingers, and close my eyes, feeling its temperature.

"Get in."

I let out a sigh when I hear his voice behind me.

I enter the bathtub, and Fazza extends his hand to steady me. He then joins me, and we sit down.

I sit between his legs, resting my head on his chest, and exhale with difficulty as he grabs a sponge to wash my belly.

I close my eyes instinctively, feeling every part of my body surrender to this man.

Fazza makes me turn towards him, and I open my eyes, finding his intense gaze.

I place one foot on each side of his waist.

"Close your eyes."

I do as he asks.

I smile as I feel him pouring water over my head, gently wetting my hair.

Without opening my eyes, I sense him moving, and soon his lips touch mine.

"So beautiful... I don't want to rush, I had to wait too long for this moment, so I want to savor every second," he whispers against my lips.

I deepen the kiss, wanting more of his touch.

Fazza's hand slides down my back, and I sigh as his tongue intertwines with mine, feeling a magnetic connection. I let my head fall back as he kisses down my neck, his beard causing a wonderful tingling sensation.

I move closer and feel his member touch my intimacy, which makes my body tense.

I may be enjoying his touches, but I'm scared.

"Don't think about it."

I believe he notices my body is tense.

"It's hard not to think about it," I murmur between kisses.

Fazza easily rises from the bathtub, bringing me to his lap.

"Aren't we going to dry off?" I ask as he walks towards the bed.

"Do we need to? We have a problem to solve..." He nibbles on my lip.

"Since when am I a problem?"

"Since the moment you sent me a video," he says, his eyes fixed on mine.

Fazza lays me down on the bed, and instinctively, I want to cover myself in front of his gaze.

"No, never cover yourself from me. I want you like this, without barriers." He grabs both of my wrists, pinning them above my head.

My husband kisses my forehead and then moves down to my lips, giving me a brief kiss that makes me even more pliant.

With his leg, he presses against the middle of my thighs, making me open them. He settles between them and brushes against my core.

"I could go crazy just from your scent. I'd recognize you even blind; your aroma is embedded in my soul. You've tattooed your essence on my body. I'm mad for you..." His voice is laden with lust.

"My sheikh," I murmur, my voice choked with desire.

"I'm yours, Helena."

I want to believe that, but he belongs to two other women.

I arch my body as I feel him blow on my breast, and my nipple becomes erect.

I can't hold back a moan when he circles my areola with his tongue.

Fazza sucks on my breast, releases my hand, and I run it over his back, feeling his skin on fire.

I throw my head back when he switches breasts. His fingers trail down to my core, parting my folds, making me bite my lip hard as I feel his finger slick with my intimacy.

"I need to bury myself in you," he murmurs, lifting his head.

I spread my legs wide as I watch him withdraw his hand and his member circle my entrance.

"It's going to hurt a bit." He presses firmly.

"Fazza," I murmur his name, pulling his face to mine.

His lips touch mine, and my tongue meets his, wanting to forget the pain coming from below.

I moan loudly as he enters fully, feeling as if I'm being torn apart.

I clutch his back, digging my nails into his skin.

"So tight and warm," he murmurs with his mouth close to mine. "I could live inside you."

"I'd love to host you," I murmur, opening a sly smile.

Fazza starts moving in slow, rhythmic thrusts, his lips kissing my neck, nibbling and leaving trails of desire wherever he goes.

Soon, I get used to his movements while seeking more contact.

"Can I go deeper?"

I nod, watching a smile form on his lips.

"So good."

My husband starts thrusting harder. I throw my head back and clutch the sheet tightly.

"I don't know of a more beautiful sight," he murmurs hoarsely, running his hand under my head and gripping my hair tightly. "From the first moment I saw you, I knew I wanted you like this, surrendering to me, opening yourself completely, giving me everything. I want everything... I want you, Helena, body and soul."

In his voice, there's a possessiveness I've never heard before.

I bite my lips as I feel his grip.

"Say you're mine, otherwise, I'll kill anyone who dares to come near my wife."

Fazza thrusts hard, forcefully, with possession, desire, and lust.

With his cock taking everything from me.

"I'm yours, my sheikh. Make me yours, take me, fuck me hard," I beg, moaning as I feel him bite my lip.

"Be like this only with me," he asks, wanting to control everything, even me.

I don't respond, and we don't speak anymore, as words are unnecessary at this moment.

Our bodies connect with the sound of them colliding echoing through the room.

I squeeze my eyes shut as I feel the spasms pass through my body, and I think I'm not the only one, as Fazza roars my name and jets of his liquid are released inside me.

I'm in a daze in the midst of my first sexual act.

The orgasm overtakes me, and I collapse limply on the bed, feeling my body exhausted, surrendered to him.

Fazza collapses on top of me, and his weight makes it hard for me to breathe.

He notices my discomfort and lies down beside me.

"We need a bath."

"Seriously? Let me sleep." I want to lie on my side.

"No, no. Come on, little one."

"Muslims and their habits. Will we always need to bathe after sex? What if I wake up in the middle of the night and want more?" I say, watching him stand in front of me.

He picks me up in his arms, and I spread my hand across his chest where there's only a few hairs.

"If you wake up, we'll do the same thing until you're tired." He smiles with the cheekiest grin.

"Not even a flinch!" I give him a light punch on the chest, hearing him laugh heartily.

CHAPTER THIRTEEN

Helena

"No..." I murmur in the midst of my dream.

I hear a smile from my side and open my eyes to find the room bright. I turn my face sideways and gently touch Fazza's face with the tips of my fingers, feeling his beard brush against my finger.

"Good morning," he whispers, noticing my laziness.

"Do we have to wake up so early?" I ask, closing my eyes.

"Yes, you should know you're already late, or rather, we are..."

I open my eyes and meet his intense gaze. I prop myself on my elbow, slide my hand down his neck, tracing a necklace he has there, then follow the line of his chest.

Fazza isn't a muscular man, perhaps quite average.

My fingers caress the few hairs he has there when he grabs my wrist, stopping my movement.

"We're late, Helena."

I lift my face at his reprimanding tone and then raise my hand in surrender. I sit up in bed, bringing a sheet with me to cover my bust and rub my eye.

I notice a tunic folded at the foot of the bed; someone left a change of clothes for me.

"You're on some sort of birth control, aren't you?"

I glance at him over my shoulder.

"Yes!" I huff.

It was the first thing I was told to do after signing that damned contract. The injection needs to be renewed in three months, or rather, two, since it's been a month since I had it.

"Is this outfit for me?" I ask, feeling a bad mood take over.

"Yes, Zaya said she would show you your room."

"Oh, should we compare notes on our husband's skills in bed?" I murmur, pulling the sheet and grabbing the tunic angrily.

I head to the bathroom like a spoiled child, stomping my feet. I lock the door, look at my reflection in the mirror, and my body is marked from last night, especially on my neck.

How did I not notice when he did this?

I take a while in the bathroom, and when I'm done, I put on my clothes, finishing with the hijab to cover my neck.

I meet my eyes in the mirror with a brighter shade of green. As much as I don't want to admit it, I liked being in Fazza's arms.

Hell!

I turn my back on myself as I leave the bathroom.

"Do you know where my phone is?" I ask somewhat rudely.

Fazza, who is buttoning up his cuffs, looks up at me.

"It should be in your room; your things were all organized there."

"Thanks," I murmur, quickly assessing his navy blue dress pants and white shirt.

"Did you lose something?" His voice is laced with mockery.

"Oh, come on..."

"I see you didn't wake up in a good mood, wife. May I know why?" he says, coming toward me.

"Depends, I could make a list." I cross my arms, looking up at him.

"So it's more than one?" He raises his eyebrow in that way I love.

Fazza touches my cheek with the tips of his fingers, and I briefly close my eyes as his lips touch mine softly.

"Shall we have breakfast?" His voice is rough.

I agree, even though I don't want to leave the room.

Fazza places his hand on my back, guiding me out of the room as I admire the beauty of the place.

He doesn't say anything, and laughter can be heard echoing through the palace.

We descend the last step. Fazza guides me down a corridor and we enter the dining room, finding his family already gathered there.

His wives, mother, brothers, and other people I don't know.

"Good morning, brother, Helena," Khalil is the first to speak, being friendly.

Everyone follows suit shortly after.

Fazza sits at the end of the table, but not before pulling out a chair for me next to Zaya and across from Samira.

Our breakfast is served, and since I am feeling down, I won't say anything unless spoken to.

"Can I ask you a question, sister-in-law?"

I look towards the man, Fazza's brother, whose name I believe is Omar.

"Go ahead," I finally say.

"You're twenty-three, right?"

I nod.

"At your age, you must have some degree; foreign women always do."

I can sense a hint of envy in his voice.

"Yes, I do. I have a degree in economic sciences." I raise an eyebrow, wanting to know the reason for his curiosity.

"I hope you don't feel entitled to comment on the economy of our country." He gives a mocking smile, as if I were nothing more than a gold digger.

I take the napkin from the table, run it through my fingers, take a deep breath, and finally say:

"Although I don't agree with everything I see, I know my duties. Rest assured, the last thing I want is to interfere in 'your' economy." I

IN THE SHEIKH'S GRASP

give a forced smile, watching the man's expression wilt in response to my answer.

I know I should keep quiet, but he can go to hell...

I blink a few times, look to the side, and see Khalil wiping his mouth to hide a smile. I can't help it; I lower my face and mimic his gesture.

During the meal, my mother-in-law didn't make any funny comments towards me. Fazza didn't speak to me; he only talked with Samira, inquiring about how the pregnancy is going. She responded with great pride that their baby boy is growing up healthy.

"If everyone will excuse me, I'll take Helena to see her room," Zaya says, looking in my direction. "Shall we?"

If I could, I would thank her for this act.

I walk beside her, but before leaving the room, I glance one last time at Fazza, who has a smile on his lips as he talks with his mother and Samira, giving them his full attention.

Is it always going to be this way, with me being the chosen one only in his bed?

I feel a tightness in my chest.

How can I be falling for a man who only sees me as a sexual object?

"We have much to discuss, Helena," Zaya interrupts my thoughts, whispering beside me. "You need to know everything, including about the baby that the viper is expecting, which is not a boy. Everyone got it wrong; the junior bride is you. You'll give our sheikh a son, and I want to be alive to see the viper Samira's defeat!"

I look at Zaya.

"That's impossible, Zaya. The baby she's expecting is a boy, and I'm not going to have children with Fazza."

CHAPTER FOURTEEN

Helena

Fortunately, Zaya forgot about the topic and shows me my room.

In the room, I find numerous jewels that Fazza gave me, as well as my new clothing.

"Can I ask you a question, Zaya?" I ask, stepping out of my closet and finding the woman standing at the door of the room.

"Yes, go ahead."

"Why are you being nice to me? I ask because of the way Samira treats me, unlike you."

Zaya falls silent, closes the door, and approaches me, whispering:

"I know you are a good woman, Helena, I can see that in you. But be careful with Samira; before you arrived, she was doing everything to make Fazza break our marriage. She wanted to be the only wife, which didn't happen, and now it's more difficult because we have you," she concludes and heads towards the door, opening it again. "You need to be alert; she gets whatever she wants around here," she says so quietly that I almost can't hear her.

I DIDN'T SEE FAZZA for the rest of the day.

I hear soft music in the corridor and follow the sound.

I'm avoiding any encounters with my mother-in-law.

Soon, childish laughter fills the room, and I see it's Fazza's daughters.

I stop in front of the open door and see the girls dancing. Zaya is with the daughters, holding a little girl in her lap.

"Come in, Helena," Safira calls me, gesturing with her hand. "Can you dance?"

"No, but I'm a quick learner. Will you teach me?"

Layla, the middle daughter, and her sister pull me into the dance.

"Safira, close the door so we have privacy for Helena to take off her hijab."

The girl runs to close the door.

Since we live in a house with many men who are not my family, I need to wear the hijab, and even though I haven't converted to Islam, I'm following their culture.

I remove the cloth from my head, and my hair falls in waves down my back.

"You're so beautiful, Helena," Layla says, taking my hand.

I dance with the two girls until Zaya gets up from the sofa with the baby, and the little girl gives a lovely toothless smile.

"May I?" I ask for permission to take the baby.

The mother agrees, handing me Jamile.

Her chubby fingers immediately reach for my hair as I join the two girls, dancing with Jamile in my lap.

"It seems you have a knack with children." Zaya smiles as she sees her daughter in my lap.

"Just your impression." I return the smile.

We spend a few minutes dancing; Layla and Safira are great teachers.

I hold Jamile's little head as she starts to show signs of drowsiness.

It feels so strange to be holding my husband's daughter in my lap.

"Do you want me to take her?" Zaya asks kindly.

I shake my head in denial, smiling.

I analyze Zaya, who is without her hijab; she has black hair that falls to the middle of her back, and since she's wearing a tunic, I don't know the shape of her body, but her features are pretty. Unlike Samira, Zaya is darker-skinned.

I lay Jamile on my lap. She has slightly almond-shaped eyes, long black lashes, and many features of her mother.

I find myself wondering what it would be like to have a child of my own with him.

What would our mix look like?

I'm startled when the door opens, and I believe Zaya feels the same as I do, because she quickly grabs her hijab.

I breathe a sigh of relief when I see it's Fazza. His gaze quickly finds mine before moving to his daughter in my lap.

"Can you give her to me?" Zaya asks, finishing putting on her hijab.

"Sure, Zaya," Fazza says with a soft voice as he enters the room. "Take Safira and Layla for a bath. I'll stay here with Helena until Jamile wakes up."

Zaya agrees, looking at me with a smile, and leaves with the two girls.

Fazza closes the door as soon as the girls leave and locks it, preventing anyone from entering.

"I don't want to risk someone coming in and seeing my wife without her hijab."

"It's just hair," I murmur, rolling my eyes.

"It's not just hair; it's mine. Everything about you belongs to me, Helena."

I can't help but scoff.

Fazza is still damp from a shower, wearing a white tunic, and his bare feet drag on the floor.

I walk to a sofa and sit down with the baby in my lap, who doesn't even stir with my movements.

Fazza sits next to me.

"Feeling better?" he asks, referring to my outburst this morning.

"As long as you stay away from the other one," I murmur.

"Samira?"

"Yes, her."

"She's pregnant and nothing should stress her out. If you can, don't do anything to upset her."

I look at him, unsure whether to open my mouth or keep it shut, not believing he's saying this.

"Don't worry, I'll stay away from your little princess," I murmur, stroking the baby's hair as she starts to sweat even though we're in an air-conditioned room.

"Helena!" Fazza says my name authoritatively.

"From the beginning, I made it clear that I wasn't sure if I could accept the fact that you have more than one wife." I raise my eyes to meet his intense black ones.

"Yes, but for now, I'm only going to bed with you."

"Of course, just for one night."

"Can you stop keeping your guard up?" he finally asks.

I remain silent.

"Helena?"

"Fine, whatever."

"Understand that I will always give everything equally to all three of you and will never let you lack for anything."

I close my eyes as I feel his touch on my cheek.

"Yes, but if you want me completely? And if you want everything? I'll never have you entirely; I will always have to share my husband."

Fazza huffs in frustration, and I can see he's lost his patience.

Something I've noticed is that he loses his patience easily.

"I'm tired; you don't need to come to my room tonight."

"But I thought..." I open my eyes to look at him.

"You thought wrong. I'm starting to realize that maybe our marriage was a mistake. You don't understand that this is who I am." Fazza gets up, running his hand through his hair.

"And this is who I am!" I retort.

I won't lower my head to him, even though I like being in his arms.

"Is this it then? You'd rather stay with this nonsense than be in my bed?" he asks, standing in front of me.

I pause a moment before finally responding:

"I'd prefer to be in your bed." My voice comes out as a whisper.

Fazza doesn't smile, just looks at me seriously.

"Then come to my room. You'll sleep with me, and don't forget to bring a tunic."

"Do the other two also spend the night with you?" I ask without thinking.

Fazza gives a forced smile, as if he can't believe what I'm asking.

"You're really something, aren't you?" He shakes his head. "No, you're the only one who sleeps with me; I always send the others back to their rooms."

The baby opens her sleepy eyes, and Fazza notices, picking her up in his arms. I smile seeing how easily he handles the baby.

I admit the scene makes me a bit giddy; he's so affectionate with the waking child.

CHAPTER FIFTEEN

Fazza

I sit on the sofa next to my two present brothers, Omar and Khalil.

It doesn't take long before I see my mother walk through the door with Samira, and I gesture for her to sit next to me. My second wife sits beside me, and her subtle fragrance fills my senses. It's pleasant, but nothing compared to Helena's; I know no woman more intriguing and fragrant than her.

"How was your day, my sheikh?" she asks with a sweet voice.

"Good, nothing out of the ordinary," I murmur.

I turn my face towards her, and her honey-colored eyes analyze me. Samira has always been a good wife, following all my orders and questioning nothing.

Everything is very easy with her, including sex.

She is modest and always asks for it to be in the dark, everything very automatic.

I lift my eyes as I sense Helena's presence in the room and quickly analyze her features. She looks at me, her eyes half-closed as if she could kill me with her hands at any moment.

After a few minutes, Helena is still gazing at me with that eagle-like look.

It's impossible not to find this woman beautiful.

She is perfect and even more alluring in bed. I'm having to hold back to give attention to all my wives when all I really want is to be with her.

"If you'll excuse me, I'm going to leave," Helena says, getting up from the sofa.

I watch her leave and soon follow, withdrawing myself.

I walk down the hallway, go up a few flights of stairs, and stop in front of my door.

I hope Helena doesn't forget to come to my room.

I turn the doorknob and enter, noticing the light is on at a low brightness, which seems odd. I hear the shower being turned off, and soon the door opens, revealing my sweet wife.

Helena looks like a sex goddess; her body is perfect, her skin has a natural tan, so smooth it makes me want to kiss every part of it.

Her green eyes are slightly slanted, and her dark brown hair is tied up in a loose bun.

My wife looks at me with eyes full of desire as her hand lifts, undoing the knot of her towel, letting it fall to the floor.

I swallow hard as I see her pointed breasts and walk towards her. My hands itch with the desire to touch her.

"You'll get this with one condition," she says with a voice thick with desire, holding my wrists to prevent me from touching her.

"And what would that be?"

"Forget everything else and let's be just you and me..."

"Just tonight?" I ask, seeing her nod.

Helena releases my hand, takes hold of the fabric of my tunic, pulls it over my head, and I'm partially nude in front of her.

Her fingers brush across my chest; her touch is soft and brings wonderful sensations to my body. I lower my face as she stands on her tiptoes, trying to kiss me. Our lips meet, and I raise my hand, letting her hair fall through my fingers, feeling the softness of her strands.

I suck on her tongue, which is sweet and tempting. I could spend an entire night just devouring those lips.

Her lips trail down, leaving light kisses on my chest until I see her kneeling in front of me. Her fingers glide along the waistband of my underwear, pulling it down.

My penis appreciates the freedom.

"Fuck, Helena..." I curse as I see her awkwardly grasp my member.

"I'm impressed you know how to use dirty words, husband." She raises only her eyes with a sly smile, running her tongue around her lip.

It's been so long since anyone has done this that I feel like a child receiving candy, yearning for the delicious touch.

"How do I do it?" she asks innocently.

I hold her hair, gripping the back of her neck.

"Suck me, go as far as you can, and avoid using your teeth as it might hurt. Circle the head of my cock with your tongue."

She nods, biting the corner of her lip.

"Like a popsicle?" she murmurs with desire.

"The most addictive one."

My wife moves closer, and I almost pass out from feeling her perfect tongue around the head of my cock. Helena takes my member into her mouth, and her lips envelop it perfectly.

She makes slow, torturous back-and-forth movements, bringing me to the height of my pleasure.

"Use your tongue, suck me, Helena," I plead with a hoarse voice.

Like a compliant girl, she does.

"Fuck..." I groan as she starts flicking her tongue around my member.

"Am I doing it right, husband?" she asks, licking all over my member as if it were a popsicle.

Her green eyes exude desire as she looks at me.

"You want to drive me crazy for you, don't you?" My voice is raspy.

"I hope I am..."

Helena goes back to sucking me, this time faster as I begin to push her head, going deeper, seeing her gag with her eyes raised towards mine. I can see the moment she gets tears in her eyes from the journey to her throat.

I don't stop and thrust deeply into her mouth, watching my goddess suck me off.

"Fuck, I'm going to cum" I say, ejaculating deep into her throat, making her swallow everything.

Helena coughs, swallowing it all, and I pull her by the arms, pressing our lips together in an urgent kiss, our teeth clashing.

Hell!

I'm crazy about this sharp-tongued woman.

I take my goddess into my lap, heading to the bed, throwing her onto the white sheets, and roughly turn her onto all fours.

"Stick that ass up for me."

She does as I ask, glancing at me from the side.

"Helena, my pleasure princess, I want to fuck you in every possible way."

I give her ass a slap, seeing it turn red, then I lower myself, kissing her butt where I had just struck. With my hands, I spread her cheeks and run my tongue, hearing her sigh. I trail my tongue from her anus down to her hot, pulsing pussy that is begging for my cock.

I lift my penis, brushing it against her entrance and insert it into the warm walls of her pussy.

I close my eyes in pleasure.

Helena is tight and appetizing.

She is surrendered and at the peak of her ecstasy.

My cock crashes hard inside her, and I grip her waist.

"Fuck!" I let out as she starts bouncing her ass on my pelvis.

Shit!

This woman is literally one of a kind.

My greedy cock takes all of her, and from the corner of my eye, I see my wife biting her lips with such force, moaning loudly.

Pleasure sounds that I love to hear coming from her mouth.

"Fazza..." she whispers, rolling her eyes.
Fuck!
I can't take it and cum again.
What does this woman have that makes me release so easily?
I am literally lost.
What is the effect she has on me?

CHAPTER SIXTEEN

Helena

I **stop** in front of the mirror and put on my hijab.

I woke up alone in Fazza's room and I don't know if he had to leave.

After finishing getting ready, I leave the room with my phone in hand, waiting for a message from my sister.

I go down the stairs, hearing laughter coming from the dining room, where they must be having breakfast.

I follow the sound into the room and see that Fazza's place is empty; he's probably not at home.

I pull out my chair and wish everyone present a good morning.

"I keep wondering when the charm will wear off."

I lift my gaze towards Samira.

When Fazza isn't around, she makes sure to throw jabs.

I swallow her affront, considering she is pregnant and I don't want to be the cause of any trouble.

"As soon as our boy is born, he will come back to you," my mother-in-law says affectionately to Samira.

I almost feel like vomiting at such flattery, so I prefer to eat in silence.

Zaya also says nothing; we stay quiet to avoid confronting the two shrews.

I finish eating and notice that the table is already partially empty. I look to the side, feeling the perfume lingering in the air.

Fazza enters wearing a white tunic with some golden accessories.

"Have you finished eating, Helena?" he asks, stopping next to me.

"Yes, I was about to get up."

"Then come with me. We're going to my stud farm; I want to show you my racehorses."

I smile, taking the hand he extends.

Fazza doesn't let go of the tip of my finger, guiding me to the outside of the house. On the way, we don't encounter his wives or his mother.

I'm relieved to leave the palace, especially with him.

A man is waiting next to a golden car.

The car is gold-plated!

I blink a few times.

The gold shines so much it almost dazzles.

I once read about the car collection owned by the Emir of Agu Dhami, but I didn't think it was real.

The man opens the passenger door.

Fazza gestures for me to sit next to the driver while he walks around and sits behind the wheel.

"I didn't know you drove." I raise an eyebrow.

Fazza gives a half-smile, starts the car, and a powerful roar echoes.

"I have my moments of fun."

I look at his hand gripping the steering wheel as we circle the fountain.

"Your fun is quite unique," I murmur, noticing a black car following us in the rearview mirror. "Now all you need to tell me is that you have a lion somewhere."

Fazza tilts his head and a sly smile appears on his lips.

"Ali and Aziz are my little cats." He shrugs.

"Oh, no! You're not joking, do you really have them? I thought it was forbidden under the new laws."

Fazza glances quickly in my direction, accelerating the car's engine.

"I stopped taking them out in the cars, nothing against keeping them. I have them and I don't give them up."

"Crazy!" I look through the car window.

"Everyone keeps what they find most fun," Fazza retorts with a smirk.

"Of course, very conventional, having a feline as a pet. Your life must be quite boring to have such hobbies." I turn my face towards my husband, who still has a smile on his face.

"My life has been quite lively these past few months."

"Your sarcastic side is a gem, my sheikh" I murmur, briefly meeting his black eyes.

"Mine?" He narrows his eyes.

"A miscalculation." I look away, facing forward as we drive towards an area with trees.

I feel Fazza's hand on my leg; his grip is firm but soon becomes gentle.

"Know that you are mine, and there's no calculation involved, just possession."

"Tell me, what do you not consider possession?" I shrug to show my displeasure.

"Welcome to my world, where I rule according to my needs and desires. Especially when it comes to you, my property."

I don't say anything, crossing my arms and taking a deep breath, feeling his scent permeate my mind, the same essence that drives me to delirium.

We pass through an entrance where the gate is already open, and a small red dirt road stretches before us, with Fazza accelerating and raising dust.

I look to the side and see a white fence, the kind I only saw in movies, and a green lawn where the horses graze.

He takes a cobblestone path and I spot a long stable with several doors where the horses' enclosures must be.

The sheikh slows down, turning off the car as he parks in a spot.

I watch him grab aviator sunglasses from the car holder and I scoff, seeing how handsome he looks even wearing those damn sunglasses. I open the car door, feeling the morning heat on my face.

I'm grateful for wearing these clothes that cover me entirely; the tunic I'm wearing is comfortable and its fabric is cool.

Fazza meets me at the front of the car.

Soon, the staff approaches and the sheikh talks directly with the manager of the stud farm, guiding us to where they train the horses in a covered ranch.

The men speak quickly and I can barely follow their dialogue in their language.

Fazza remains by my side, showing no affection, not even holding my hand, which is normal in their culture.

We enter the area where two horses are training and men are shouting at the animals.

No one says anything to me or even looks at me; it's as if I don't exist, all out of respect for their emir.

We stop in front of the enclosure that separates the training arena and I watch a black horse with a man riding it.

Upon noticing the emir's presence, he trots over to us. The man stops in front of us and removes his protective helmet.

I furrow my brow as I look at his features.

I know him from somewhere...

Then I remember, it's Kaled.

He's the one who helped me get Nain's email.

Now it all makes sense; he works for the sheikh, not directly, but he does work for him.

"Kaled?" I call his name, drawing everyone's attention to me.

CHAPTER SEVENTEEN

Helena

Great, I messed up!
Since when does a woman call a man like that?
Kaled looks at me in desperation.
"Do you know him?" Fazza asks in a serious tone.
And now, what should I say?
I don't want to harm Kaled; after all, he was the one who helped me, even though he disappeared after I came to the Emirates.
"Helena?" My husband asks again.
I look at my social media friend, and he shrugs.
"We only know each other through the internet, Emir."
Fazza turns back to the boy and then grips my arm tightly.
Without saying a word, he pulls me as if I were an object.
"You're hurting me," I complain, wanting him to let me go.
My husband ignores my plea and we exit through the side door, where there are several stables. He leads me to one, shoving me into the empty stall and I feel the hay beneath my feet.
"Fazza, this isn't what you think," I say as soon as we're alone.
I look around at the exposed bricks and, surprisingly, the place doesn't smell bad.
"What am I thinking, Helena?"
I gulp as I see him walk towards me, pinning me against the wall while his hand holds my wrists above my head.

"I don't know what you're thinking," I murmur, finding his eyes very close to mine.

"I'll kill the man who dares to say a word to you without my consent."

His voice has a possessive tone, as if he wants to control my entire life.

"It's not the *fuck* you're thinking! Let me explain and stop jumping to conclusions," I say, losing my patience, confronting him.

"Then speak, Helena..."

"I met Kaled when I still lived in Brazil. We only communicated through messages, and he always knew about my fascination with the Emirates. He's the one who got Nain's email, and part of the reason I'm here today is because of him."

Fazza remains silent; our breaths are quick and my chest has a frantic rhythm of rising and falling.

Without warning, his mouth devours mine, in a desire for possession, as if he wants to mark my soul, more than it's already marked.

His tongue enters my mouth, in a slow dance, and the kiss that was urgent turns into something calm and erotic.

Fazza releases my wrists, holding my waist firmly.

I reach for his neck, feeling the tips of his hair in a soft touch.

"Say that you're mine?" he murmurs amid the kiss, sucking my lip.

"Make me yours, here, now," I beg, opening my eyes, pleading with him.

Fazza lowers his lips down my neck and easily removes my hijab, letting it fall on the dry straw.

"Fuck, Helena, this goes against all my principles. I want your moans and sighs only for myself. You'll have to control yourself to stay silent."

I agree, turning my back, rubbing my butt against his erect member under his tunic.

Easily, I lift my hips and Fazza grips my bare buttocks, pulling my panties down and tearing them.

I bite my lip.

My husband lifts his tunic and takes me from behind.

I look sideways as his free hand grabs my hair.

I sigh, feeling his cock take me forcefully.

"If you can't control yourself, I'll stop. No one can hear you. You are mine, and everything about you belongs to me. Every moan, sigh, bite of that delicious little mouth... You are mine, every inch of you is mine! Even if it's just for a damned contract."

His voice is hoarse and laden with desire.

I can't say anything, just biting my thumb trying to control my moans.

Fazza lowers his hand to my intimacy, stimulating my clitoris while penetrating me in a delicious rhythm.

I briefly close my eyes, feeling my walls opening up to him as I grind against his cock, wanting all of him.

I never thought sex could be this good.

Or is it him who makes everything more enjoyable?

"Fazza..." I murmur, rolling my eyes.

His fingers keep moving and his cock increases the pace, taking all of my pussy.

The sounds of our bodies start echoing in the tiny stable.

"Oh, my sheikh" I whisper, delirious for my husband.

Spasms run through my body and my walls constrict around his member.

"Fazza" I call his name as an orgasm courses through every cell of my being.

My husband comes with me, embracing my body from behind, and I feel his sweat on my neck as he rests his head against me.

We stay like this for long seconds until he pulls out and I feel the emptiness left by his cock.

I turn my body to face my sheikh, closing my eyes as I feel his hand caressing my cheek, tucking my hair behind my ear.

"So perfect..."

I open my eyes to find his dark orbs.

"Can we sit?"

"Here?" He asks, surprised.

"Yes, here, on the hay, like a normal couple who sits down to rest. I don't think anyone will disturb the sheikh," I murmur with a forced smile.

Fazza crouches, sitting on the ground and then calls me to sit on his lap.

"A normal couple?" He asks as I settle on his lap, feeling his chest against my head.

"Yes, sometimes I miss that," I murmur, yawning.

"I don't know if I'll ever be able to give you that, this is my world." His hand moves to my temple and massages my head.

I remain silent, just listening to our breathing.

"Fazza, I don't know if I'll be able to handle seeing you go to bed with any of your women. I won't be able to, it's too much for me," I whisper, trying to erase any thoughts of Zaya or Samira from my mind.

"Let's not think about that now..." He murmurs, wanting to change the subject.

"I wish it were that simple." I huff, seeing him sigh in disgust.

"When that happens, you'll be the first to know, because it won't be you in my bed at night."

Automatically, my eyes burn and my heart tightens in my chest, as if the space had become too small to pump.

I fight against my tears, trying not to suffer in advance.

I can't share my husband, I definitely can't.

I know that when that moment comes, I'll suffer too much, and I don't know if I'll be able to go to bed with him again after that.

CHAPTER EIGHTEEN

Fazza

"Have Kaled called," I ask Nain as soon as we return to the horse training.

Helena is beside me, impatient, so I hold the tip of her finger, wanting minimal contact with her.

"Please, Fazza, don't be unfair to him," my wife pleads in a whisper.

Out of the corner of my eye, I see her lips slightly swollen from the number of kisses I gave her sensitive skin, while her green eyes are still shining from the pleasure we shared minutes ago.

Being with Helena has been good for me; I feel like a teenager and want her all the time. I've never allowed myself such irresponsibility by having sex practically in public, but in my defense, she persuaded me.

How could I say no to such a request?

How could I say no to this sexy woman?

She has the most beautiful and enticing curves I've ever experienced. When I'm with her, I feel like I can do anything; it's as if this little enchantress is testing me all the time, and I, enchanted, let myself be led.

I lift my eyes as I see the two men approaching and ask everyone around us to leave us alone.

I see the man who helped Helena; he must be her age, and his expression is frightened.

"Emir." He gives a brief greeting.

"How did you get Nain's email?" I go straight to the point.

"What do you mean?" My assistant interjects, not knowing what this is about.

"Please, Fazza, I've already said he's not to blame," Helena says with a sweet voice.

"It wasn't hard to get; I went into the stud office and found Mr. Nain's email there," the man says, looking down.

"So you mean it was through him that you got the address to send the videos?" Nain asks with wide eyes.

"Yes, sir. I helped Helena, but I didn't do it out of malice. We had a friendship and I liked talking to her. Helena always spoke of her passion and fascination for the Emirates, and I just wanted to help her. I never imagined she would become a princess of Agu Dhami. But as soon as I knew you had invited her to visit you, I cut all ties with her."

Kaled glances briefly at Helena, making me want to remove his eyes.

Helena is mine, and no one should look at her with desire.

From the boy's tone, it's clear that he wanted her and was doing everything he could to have her.

But she is mine!

Helena is destined to spend the rest of her life by my side.

I take a deep breath, feeling my wife's fingers interlace with mine in a silent plea to let the young man go without any warning.

"Just because you brought my princess, I'll let you go without any reprimand. I hope never to hear any further offense from you and stay away from the royal family, especially from my wife," I say, seeing the three of them sigh at my words.

I am a very good emir; I always prioritize the well-being of my people and like to provide everyone with the comfort I have.

Our Emirate is an example of grandeur and wealth.

But in the midst of all this, I am controlling and like to have everything in the palm of my hand. I need to control everyone's lives, especially my junior wife, my little treasure found by chance and now my downfall.

No one can even think of Helena, and if I find out, I'll kill.

I look to the side, and Helena's gaze is fixed on me.

"Shall we go?" I ask, wanting to leave the place.

She agrees, walking beside me, followed by a few men.

I spot my *Lamborghini*.

"I've always wanted to drive a car like this, can I?"

"Are you serious?" I ask, searching for a hint of teasing in her voice and not finding any.

"Please?" She clasps her hands together, pouting in a way I want to bite.

I huff; I'm not very attached to material possessions, as I can always renew them.

"Go ahead then, let's see how you do."

Helena lets out a happy little laugh as she heads toward the driver's seat. I walk around the car and sit in the passenger seat.

I instruct her on how to start the car, and my wife follows with attention. The engine roars, and she looks in the rearview mirror as she backs up.

"You know you can't drive here, right? You don't have our credentials."

"Oh, it's fine, I have the highest order by my side." A smile forms on her lips.

"Exactly for that reason, we need to set an example," I murmur, sliding my hand under her hijab and feeling the skin of her neck.

"Fazza, don't distract me." She sighs, her eyes fixed on the road.

"I love hearing my name spoken by your lips."

Helena lets out a smile.

"Follow the black car; it's one of our security guards."

She nods.

As Helena drives, I keep my hand on her neck, massaging it and listening to her sigh occasionally.

I take my phone from the car mount and see a video message from Zaya. I play the video and smile as I see my youngest daughter taking her first steps.

Jamile smiles as her chubby little legs walk across the playroom.

"Is that Jamile?" Helena asks, hearing my daughter's laughter echoing in the car.

"Yes, Zaya sent a video of her taking her first steps."

"Oh, how cute, I need to see those little sausage legs walking through the room," Helena says with affection.

"Do you like children, Helena?" I ask, watching her gaze meet mine before she turns her eyes back to the road.

I judge that she hadn't really thought about it, responding immediately.

"My dream is to one day become a mother, to be better than my birth mother was when she abandoned me in that orphanage," she says thoughtfully.

All I can think is that I would never want to have a child with her. It's not that I don't want children with her, but I'm selfish and only want her for myself.

CHAPTER NINETEEN

Helena

I yawn and stretch as I sit on the bed, seeing the empty space beside me.

Fazza must have already left; he wakes up early for his prayer and soon goes to handle some matters at the palace.

I grab my robe from the sheets, always bringing a clean piece to wear the next morning.

I hold the fabric in my hand, look at the messy bed, and find myself thinking about the day when I won't be warming his sheets. My chest quickly contracts with a pain that I know I will endure.

I sigh as I put on the robe over my underwear and bra, the wine-colored fabric adorned with small gems that add delicate details to the piece.

I head to the bathroom, brush my long hair, and braid it, tucking it behind my hijab.

With one last look in the mirror, I leave the room and walk down the corridor.

I hear laughter coming from the living room and follow the sound.

Sometimes, I miss privacy and wonder how they manage it.

As I descend the final flight of stairs, I turn away from the dining room and enter the central room where everyone in the family is. They must have already had breakfast.

I enter quietly, going unnoticed, and am not surprised to find Samira next to Fazza.

"Fazza always has good taste," she says, holding a necklace around her neck. "I love it, my sheikh."

He doesn't say anything.

He must have given a gift to his second wife, I think, until I see that Zaya has a similar necklace; he gave gifts to both of them.

"Did you get one too, Helena?" Samira notices my presence.

My gaze briefly meets the honey-colored eyes of the second wife.

"No," I murmur.

The room falls silent, and I can't look at Fazza; I can't look at him when he's next to this woman, it feels like a betrayal.

"Don't be foolish, Samira."

I turn my face towards Zaya, who mocks as she speaks.

"Helena doesn't need that; she is being rewarded in another way."

Zaya leaves Samira speechless; she understood what the first wife meant.

The tense atmosphere is broken when Nain enters the room with his wife, Isa.

"Isa" Samira pretends to forget, greeting the woman cheerfully.

"Hello, Samira. The baby is growing healthily in your womb," Isa says.

"Our boy," the woman says affectionately about her son.

"Or girl," Zaya murmurs. "We can't forget that the junior wife is now someone else."

"By Allah, Zaya!" Fazza scolds.

Zaya lowers her head.

"I came to see if Helena wants to join me for shopping," Isa says, drawing my attention.

"Oh!" Samira exclaims in disappointment.

"May I go with her?" Isa asks my husband.

I can't help but look at him now; we're at a long distance, and his black eyes meet mine.

We stay like that for long seconds, our connection almost palpable.

"It's fine with me..." he finally says.

"Shall we go, Helena?"

I break the contact with the sheikh, looking at my friend.

"You don't have to ask twice." I wink at her.

"Can I come too?" Safira asks, getting up from the sofa.

"Daughter" Zaya calls the girl's attention.

"It's fine with me, as long as your parents allow it." I shrug.

"Dad, can I go?" she asks her father.

Fazza gets up from the sofa, where he was sitting next to Samira.

"Behave, Safira."

The girl jumps with joy.

"First, let's get changed, daughter," Zaya calls her daughter's attention.

"Can I go, Zaya?" I ask.

She raises an eyebrow in surprise at my request but soon smiles and agrees.

"I'll come too," Isa joins me. "After all, we have a lot to talk about."

I extend my hand to Safira, and the girl grabs my fingers with a huge smile.

Since I arrived, Isa has been my friend, and our connection is very strong. She is the best friend I could have dreamed of.

"Let me fix your hair since mine always has to be covered," I offer to Safira, who happily nods.

I glance briefly at Fazza, and his eyes have a different sparkle, something I can't decipher.

We head towards the stairs and climb the steps.

"HOW ARE THINGS WITH the sheikh?" Isa murmurs beside me while Safira looks at a display window.

"He's controlling, as if I were his property," I whisper.

"It's normal among our Arab men; they have that possessive feeling."

"The problem is that he's not mine, and I have to share him. I don't know if I'll manage, just seeing him next to one of his wives already makes something unpleasant well up inside me. I won't be able to bear the thought of him going to bed with any of them..."

Isa pats my hand.

"Nain confided in me that he's giving gifts to the other wives because he misses them. He's been sleeping by your side every night, hasn't he? Fazza has always been a man who takes traditions seriously, and I see him breaking most of them with you. He sees you as his favorite, enjoy that privilege."

I look at the girl admiring the display window with her little eyes shining.

"The problem is that I want more and will never have my husband just for me. Doesn't Nain think about marrying again?"

"No, we signed a contract. My husband gave up polygamy, and I will be his only wife."

I can't help but give a forced smile.

"I'm so jealous," I murmur, laughing.

"Helena" Safira calls me. "What do you think of this tunic?"

Isa and I approach the girl who is looking at the clothes.

"Do you want to go in?" I ask.

Safira nods enthusiastically.

I take advantage of the all-women moment and renew some pieces to my liking.

When Safira goes to check out other items, I enter the lingerie section and buy something daring, imagining my sheikh with his jaw dropped.

"You're such a naughty girl," Isa whispers in my ear, laughing.

"Everyone plays with the cards they have."

Safira begs for us to get ice cream, and we take lots of selfies with millions of poses and pouty faces.

I'm putting my phone back in my pocket when Fazza's name appears on the screen. I answer the call, placing the phone to my ear and stepping away from the girls.

"Miss me, darling?" I say before he says anything.

"You know I spend my days only thinking about my nights with you. How are things? Is Safira being a nuisance? I saw you didn't eat before leaving home, have you eaten?"

"Calm down, Fazza!" I interrupt before he continues with the questions. "Everything is fine, relax. We're having a pleasant day, and I even bought something."

"If I know you well, you're biting your lip. Do I need to remind you that only I can do that to that perfect little mouth? What did you buy?"

"Always a question after another." I can hear him smiling on the other end of the line. "It's a surprise, something that will leave my sheikh, how can I put it..." I look around and noticing no one is paying attention, I press the phone to my mouth and whisper: "With a hard-on."

I can hear him exhale heavily.

"Helena Simões, what to do with you?"

"Do you want me to tell you, husband?" I smile, ending the call, leaving him with his imagination.

I'm going to make Fazza eat out of the palm of my hand...

This Arab has messed with the wrong Brazilian.

CHAPTER TWENTY

Fazza

I leave my phone charging next to the bed and lie down, placing my hand under my head as I look up at the ceiling.

I'm impatient with Helena's delay.

My nightly routine with this woman is becoming essential; I want her every night, as if my body demands hers.

It's a habit that's overtaking my mind.

My heart only calms down when her warm body is next to mine and her breath is near mine.

I know I need to fulfill my marital duties with Zaya in the conjugal bed, but she hasn't seemed bothered. On the contrary, she's becoming more and more distant, as if pushing me into Helena's arms.

Zaya has always been very devoted; I know she accepted the marriage for her father's sake, and I try to do everything I can to make her comfortable.

With Samira, things are easier, and I know that when we have our child, she will fulfill her role as a wife.

I close my eyes.

I will have to take Samira to bed when our child is born, and I have no doubt about that; she has made it clear that she wants this house full of our children.

But how can I do that when the only woman dominating my thoughts is Helena?

It's as if my body desires and wants only hers.

I'm pulled from my thoughts when I hear the noise of the door; with a knock, I see my wife entering the room.

"You're late." I sit up in bed, folding my leg with the white sheet covering my body.

Helena removes her hijab, letting her long hair fall on her shoulder, and I sigh at the delicacy of the strands framing her face.

"I was busy."

Her voice is a soft whisper that excites me.

I swallow hard as I watch her tunic fall to her feet as she removes it.

I squint as I analyze the lingerie she's wearing while she walks slowly towards me. Her breasts are covered by a bra with partially transparent fabric, leaving the nipples exposed. I let my eyes travel down her smooth belly to her pussy, which seems to beg for my fingers, my mouth.

The red lingerie makes me want to rip it off and devour every inch of her body.

Helena stops in front of me, and her green eyes are shining with the lust her body exudes.

"Can I know what my wife was busy with?" I ask, seeing her bite her lips.

"I wanted to look good for you," she murmurs.

I remove the sheet from my body and sit at the edge of the bed, making Helena stand in the middle of my legs.

"More desirable than you already are? Impossible! I don't know a more desirable woman than you..."

I lose myself in smelling her belly, and her rose scent floods my mind. My hand travels down her waist, grabs the thin fabric of her panties, and easily tears it, wanting her smooth pussy for myself.

"Fazza, my new lingerie," Helena says with a squeak.

"I could buy millions of these, one for every night you're by my side," I say, squeezing her ass.

Her buttocks are so soft, they feel like two cushions I want to squeeze, bite, spank, and see turn red with pleasure.

My tongue circles her navel, going to her spot that I sniff strongly, soon letting my tongue invade her folds.

Helena sighs heavily.

I see she's limp and surrendered to the moment, so I take the opportunity to lie down.

I hold her hand.

"Bring that pussy to my mouth for me to enjoy," I ask, watching her blush.

Helena complies, crawling over my body until her spot is over my face.

I hold her thighs, squeezing them tightly, keeping her open for me with her intimacy in my mouth, then let my tongue savor her addictive flavor.

My wife is so delicious that I could come just with her pussy rubbing against my face.

Helena can't contain herself and starts to gyrate, rubbing my mouth against her entrance.

My tongue flicks in her folds, I squeeze her ass while my finger outlines her little anus, which I will have.

I hear Helena moaning, writhing, until her body releases spasms into my mouth. Like little shocks, she gives herself up, and I suck her with eagerness.

She tries to get off me, but I stop her, making her sit on my lap with my hard cock like a rock between us.

"Grind for me, real nice..." I ask, pulling her mouth into a kiss.

I grab her hair tightly, and my wife moans.

"Like this? Like this?" she asks with a hoarse voice and a naughty smile on her face.

Helena starts rubbing her pussy on my cock, increasing my desire to penetrate her, to fuck my wife hard.

"That's it..." I say, feeling her sit on my member, her walls taking me in. — *"Fuck..."*

I bring her lips to mine, kiss her mouth, and devour her tongue.

A moan escapes from my mouth, feeling her ride my cock.

She grinds like a goddess.

This woman has an immense power over me; it's as if she holds me in the palm of her hand, and I've never felt so vulnerable to anyone as I do with her.

Helena doesn't know it, but she's been winning more and more of my heart every day.

I hold her waist, making her lie down on the bed, positioning myself between her legs and resuming forceful penetration, with urgency, wanting everything from her.

"Fazza..." she moans like a cat.

Her nails scratch my back in a rhythm of urgent back-and-forth, with force.

Our bodies clash and sweat connects us.

I pull the fabric of her bra, tearing it, taking her nipple into my mouth, sucking hard, smearing her soft skin with my tongue.

Helena writhes, moans, sighs, and I take in every detail of this woman, wanting her all the time, every night.

Unable to hold on any longer, I come hard, moaning her name.

"Shit," I'm screwed!

This woman is driving me crazy.

I STEP OUT OF THE SHOWER wrapped in a towel, enter the bedroom, and see my little wife wrapped in my sheets, sleeping peacefully. Her breathing is calm, gentle, and her expression conveys tranquility and relaxation.

I set the towel aside and lie down, pulling her body close to mine.

Helena murmurs something inaudible, snuggling into my chest with her butt rubbing against my cock.

"No, Fazza."

I lift my head thinking she's awake, but she's dreaming.

"No, Fazza, no... Please." She turns, lifting her face, and looks at me frightened.

"Hey, calm down, it was just a dream," I murmur, stroking her hair.

"A bad dream, very bad." Her eyes shine with sadness.

I pull her body close to mine; she lies on my chest, her breathing, which was rapid, returns to being calm.

"I wish so much that this fear would go away, that you were only mine." My wife lifts her face and falls back asleep.

It seems she is still dreaming as she falls asleep so easily, unlike me, who is left thinking about her words.

Does Helena have fear?

Fear of seeing me go to bed with one of my other wives?

It's selfish of me, I know; I wanted her even knowing she would never accept me with other wives and that she would be eternally upset when she learns she won't be the only one in my bed.

CHAPTER TWENTY-ONE

Helena

I feel my body being suffocated, as if I were in a dream. The same dream where Fazza enters a room with Samira.

I wriggle, trying to get out, until I open my eyes and see that I'm still in his room. I look to the side and find his intense black eyes studying me.

Daybreak arrives, and the room starts to get brighter.

"You had a tense night," he murmurs.

"Did I move too much?" I ask with a hoarse voice.

"Yes, you sat up in bed several times, said something, and went back to sleep."

I huff, sitting up in bed and running my hand over my face. I usually do this when I start having anxiety attacks; it's my fear haunting my worst dreams.

I close my eyes as I feel Fazza's hand on my back. He moves my hair aside and kisses my shoulder.

"Sorry I couldn't do anything to ease your torment."

The kisses travel up to my neck, making me sigh with the caress of his beard.

"Fazza..." I turn my face. "Once you said you knew about my parents," I ask, watching him lift his eyes towards me.

His hand caresses my cheek.

"Yes..."

IN THE SHEIKH'S GRASP

I fix my eyes on his mouth, the same one that was on my intimacy last night.

"What do you know?"

"It depends, what do you want to know?"

I turn my body to face his.

Fazza moves his hand to my waist, pulling me into his lap, where I snuggle.

"I want to know everything, I don't know anything."

He studies me with his intense eyes for long seconds until he finally starts to speak:

"You were adopted at five years old, right?"

I nod, and Fazza moistens his lips, continuing:

"Your mother, Anastácia Lima, left you at the orphanage when you were two. She had problems with drugs and is now in a rehabilitation center. Her brother, Pedro Lima, is paying for the clinic. It seems to be the only family she has. As for why he never came looking for you, I don't know."

I shift my gaze to the light-colored wall.

My mother is alive, it's the only thing my brain can process.

"How did you find all this out?" I ask, looking back at him.

"It wasn't too hard. The orphanage provided all the information without question, though my detective paid a high amount."

I roll my eyes; it had to involve money.

"And my father? Do you know anything?"

Fazza holds my waist, his fingers sliding up my belly, leaving trails of fire as they pass.

"Lucas Simões, that's his name. I didn't research his life, just know that he's imprisoned for armed robbery; it seems he's in a prison in Rio de Janeiro." He furrows his brow trying to remember. "If you want, I can ask Nain to give you the file we collected."

"My parents are both fucked up," I murmur, feeling my eyes burn. "I want the file," I say finally, trying to get off his lap.

"No." He holds me tightly, pulling me back, lying down and making me lie on top of him.

His arm slides down my back, and my body shivers at his touch.

"So beautiful," he murmurs, stroking my face with his other hand. "I keep wondering what you have. Why do I desire you so much? Helena..." His voice fades, lost in some thought.

Our lips come together in a slow kiss, as if words aren't necessary, just the moment and the two of us.

Just the two of us.

The kiss becomes more erotic, his mouth sucking my lip, eventually biting it.

"Helena..." he murmurs my name like a prayer.

"Fazza, the sheikh of my dreams," I whisper, smiling, letting my eyes meet his.

"Your fascination has become mine for you." His eye is so black that the pupil is almost imperceptible. "Tell me what you want, Helena, and I'll give it to you. Tell me..."

I sigh, kissing his lip again.

Fazza shifts position, climbing on top of me, pressing me with the warmth of his chest.

"What I want, you can never give me. Not all your gold will be able to buy such a feeling."

He lifts his eyes, and his soul is so vulnerable now.

"Helena..." he murmurs.

"You don't need to say anything; from the beginning, you made it clear what you wanted from me. There's no need to confuse things." I turn my face away.

"Don't make things difficult. I want you with all my being, but I can't be only yours. I have two other wives, one of whom is pregnant."

Fazza gets off me, and I feel the cold where he was once warming me.

IN THE SHEIKH'S GRASP

I don't say anything, lying down on the opposite side of the bed from him.

Tears burn my face; I want to hide it so he doesn't see that I'm vulnerable to him.

I hear his footsteps and sit up.

How can I be so foolish?

To imagine that one day he might give them up for me.

I ignore him, grab my tunic from the foot of the bed, and put it on haphazardly. I look for the hijab and don't find it until I see Fazza holding it in his hand.

I roll my eyes seeing that he's holding it for me to take.

"Know that I want you in my bed again tonight."

I huff as I walk towards him.

I want to pull the hijab from his hand, but he repeats the gesture, pulling me into his arms.

"Helena." He lifts my face by the chin. "Nothing in this life will make me give you up. Not all my gold. You warm my bed and heat my heart, so forget any notion of divorce. I will never give you freedom; you are mine!"

"That never crossed my mind, though I'd love to be away from you. Damn day I became fascinated by this culture. I hate you, Fazza." I want to punch his chest.

He gives a mocking smile, holding my wrists.

"We both know that deep down, everything you're saying is a lie, but let's not argue about it. I hate arguments." He releases me, leaving the hijab in my hand.

"*Oh,* I actually love it. And I love it even more when I'm right. You think you're the owner of the world, don't you, Fazza?"

The sheikh, who had turned his back, turns around to look me in the eyes.

"I don't know if they told you, but here, I am in charge. Not just of you, but of the entire Emirate of Agu Dhami."

I gasp at his sarcasm and stomp out of his room.

CHAPTER TWENTY-TWO

Helena

TWO MONTHS LATER...

My duties have been nothing more than going to Fazza's bed.
After our brief argument, I found myself powerless, unable to argue against him.

I surrendered to him.

A whim made me sign the contract; a life I thought was luxurious and pure gold made me briefly blind.

I can't say I hate this place because I love it.

I love this damned sheikh and I hate myself for loving him.

Fazza is controlling, wants everything to pass before his eyes, and doesn't allow a single word to be said behind his back.

I can't get his touches out of my mind, the way he caresses me, adores me every night, his lips on my skin...

Everything drives me crazy.

I want him for myself body and soul, just for me.

But I can't...

Samira has been in labor for a few hours, and this is the first night we haven't spent together since we got married.

Fazza is with his second wife, eagerly awaiting their first male child, and I chose not to witness this scene, so I'm in my room.

I feel bad for not being happy about this child when everyone else is.

My mother-in-law hates me, always making some tasteless joke or even direct insults whenever she has the chance. All because I'm not Muslim and chose not to convert to Islam.

Fazza, who is the most important person in this whole story, doesn't care, so why should she?

I've noticed that Zaya has been lurking in the shadows of the palace as if something is bothering her...

I'm pulled from my reverie when I hear someone knock on the door. I lift my head from the pillow and hear:

"It's me, Helena, can I come in?"

To my surprise, Zaya appears knocking at my door.

"Come in, Zaya," I say, sitting up.

I don't bother putting on the hijab since we are just two women.

The first wife enters, closing the door and immediately removing her hijab.

"Sit down." I pat the bed for her to sit in front of me.

"We need to talk, Helena," she says seriously, which gives me a brief stomach churn.

"Has something happened, Zaya?" I ask, anxious.

"No, it's not about the sheikh. To be honest, I don't even know how the labor is going. It's so quiet that I wonder if the baby has already been born..."

The woman in front of me gets lost in her thoughts.

"I'm not following either. I know that with the birth of the child, Samira will have the freedom to warm Fazza's bed. — I feel my eyes fill with tears. — I'm not ready," I murmur, trying with all my might to hold back my tears.

"When I saw you come into this house, I felt in my heart that you were the right person for Fazza. I only stay here for my daughters and thank Allah every night that I no longer have to go to my husband's bed. Not that I don't like the sheikh. I might even love him, but not in the same intensity that you two love each other. It's clear what you two feel. In a room full of people, your eyes shine, and only a fool wouldn't notice... — She stops talking to hold my hand.

"Fazza is very controlling, and even if he loved only me, he would never end another marriage, just out of his own selfishness," I murmur, feeling Zaya caress my fingers.

"I've made up my mind, Helena. I'm going to ask for a divorce, and he has to give it to me. My father always said that if I wasn't happy, I could return to my family because the doors would always be open for me. I didn't make this decision before because I didn't want to leave my daughters in Samira's hands, but now that you are here, I have nothing to fear. I know you will be a good mother to them, just like I am." She lets a tear fall.

"But why, Zaya? Why don't you want to stay with the sheikh?" I ask, wanting to understand her perspective.

"When Fazza married me, it wasn't a marriage of love, after all, love is built after marriage. I always thought I could change, that my body could evolve, but no. It's always the same, I fulfill my duties as a woman out of obligation. I don't enjoy going to bed with him or any man. And before you think otherwise, I don't enjoy being with women either. I like being alone, the presence of my daughters. But I don't like going to bed; I just don't. I only went out of obligation, like it was an automatic act."

"You're an asexual person, Zaya; don't feel awful about it." I raise my hand, wiping a tear from her face.

"What is that?" She frowns.

"Asexual is a person who doesn't feel sexual attraction. They're not attracted to anyone and don't act on erotic desire. That's it. But if you look it up online, you'll find more about it."

Zaya looks at me for long seconds.

I think about how many women in this Emirate marry, even knowing that something is wrong with themselves, and don't think twice before fulfilling their duty as women.

Although things are evolving here, there are still many cases of marriages of convenience and hierarchy. This was the case with Zaya and Fazza, since he comes from a long line of sheikhs and she is a sheikha.

"Why don't you take your daughters with you? Jamile is so small," I murmur.

"I can't. My daughters need to stay with their father; he is the one who holds most of our assets. — The woman lowers her head and then continues: — Can I trust you with my girls, Helena?"

I open my mouth several times, but nothing comes out.

How do I tell her that I can barely take care of myself?

I love the three little girls and spend most of my time with them. Safira taught me to dance, Layla is cheerful, and little Jamile is just a baby full of light to share.

"Alright, I'll take care of them with all my heart, but don't think this is a goodbye, okay? We will always see each other when we can." I let a smile spread across my lips.

I lean forward, open my arms, and hug the woman in front of me.

"Wish me luck, because I still need to talk to Fazza," she says between our embrace.

CHAPTER TWENTY-THREE

Helena

The house is still in complete silence, which is strange.

Is this how they celebrate the birth of a child?

I hold onto the railing as I descend the stairs and enter the room where I find some people seated.

Seeing that everyone is scattered, I head to the courtyard where I find Safira and Layla running around.

I sit on one of the white marble benches and watch them run.

Safira, the older sister, spots me and runs in my direction.

"Hello, Helena," she says with a smile. "The new baby has arrived, we heard the crying, but we still don't know if it's a boy or a girl." She pouts, making me smile.

"Don't worry about that, we'll find out soon," I say, tucking the girl's hair behind her ear.

The girls return to running around.

After a few minutes, I get up and head to the room where I see Fazza entering.

He's wearing his white robe and his hair is damp; he must have showered.

His expression is serious.

"The baby has been born," he says, causing everyone to sigh with relief. "Mother and baby are doing well and are recovering."

"What a joy, brother." Khalil claps his hands, thanking Allah. "Now tell us, what is the name of our boy?"

The room falls into complete silence until Fazza finally breaks the tension:

"It's Aysha, a beautiful little girl."

"What?" Omar almost jumps off the couch.

"That's what you heard, my brother; it's a girl. I don't want anyone judging Samira," Fazza says authoritatively. "My wife is weak and sensitive right now, but she will have the chance to get pregnant again soon."

His words make my stomach churn, my whole body tenses, the walls start spinning, and all I can think about is that I need to find a bathroom urgently.

"By Allah, Helena..."

The last thing I hear is Zaya practically shouting, and everything goes blurry before I collapse to the floor.

SOMETHING COLD IS PLACED on my forehead, which makes me open my eyes and see Zaya and Isa looking down at me.

"What happened?" I ask, my voice a bit weak.

"You fainted, and I don't know if it was from happiness that the baby is a girl," Zaya says, laughing.

That reminds me of the moment.

"No." I close my eyes again. "It was hearing from Fazza that he and Samira will have another child, which means they'll have to share the same bed." My eyes fill with tears.

"Oh, Helena, my sweet." Isa holds my hand, sitting beside me.

"Ramadan is coming up, isn't it?" I ask.

"Yes, in a few days," Zaya replies.

"I'm going to ask to travel to my country; I'm exhausted. I miss my sister and mother, and I can't stand the pressure of knowing he'll be going to bed with Samira at any moment."

"I don't know if the sheikh will allow it," Isa murmurs.

"He has to allow it; I'm not Muslim. I don't need to observe Ramadan, and being here would only be a thorn in Fazza's side..." I say impatiently. "I need this month; I need some family comfort."

The two of them look at me; I think they see my state of exhaustion.

We are taken by surprise when the door opens and Fazza walks in.

Zaya and Isa stand up, leaving the room with a brief nod.

The sheikh closes the door and walks toward me.

"Are you feeling better?" he asks, sitting where Zaya was before.

I sit on the bed, folding my legs and hugging them.

"Yes, I'm fine," I murmur, inhaling his wonderful scent.

Fazza approaches and strokes my face, making me close my eyes and feel his touch.

"Congratulations on your daughter," I murmur, feeling him stop his touch.

I open my eyes, and Fazza looks lost.

"We all expected it to be a boy, but it's a girl. It's not that I don't love her; I love all my daughters, but I wanted to leave my Emirate to a son of mine, and I see that won't happen."

His voice has a slight disappointment.

"I don't even know what to say to you." I'm not the best person to offer him words of comfort at a time like this.

I take a deep breath and continue:

"Fazza, I want to ask you something."

He gestures for me to go on.

"I want to take advantage of Ramadan and visit my family."

"A month away?"

His reaction surprises me as I see him get up and pace back and forth.

"What difference does it make? We won't be going to bed anyway. It will be a month of reflection for you, let me go," I plead almost desperately.

"Why? Why do you want to be away from me?" he asks, crossing his arms.

"It's easy for you. You're not seeing me with another man; I am, Fazza. I am! I have to listen to you almost every day saying that you'll need to go to bed with someone else. I have to share you and feel betrayed every time I see you touching your other wives. And don't come at me with this gold gift nonsense; none of it fills the pain I feel every time I see you with them. No amount of gold can buy me when I want just one thing from you!"

My eyes burn with tears, tears of pain, not understanding the fact that he will still go to bed with Samira.

With Zaya, it's easy; she doesn't care and runs from Fazza, but Samira has made it very clear that once her baby is born, she'll take her place in his bed, and I'll be replaced.

"Shall we go back to this topic, Helena?" he huffs, exasperated.

"Let's, Fazza, let's! Because you always find a way to avoid it, to not want to talk about it." I get up from the bed and hold onto the backrest, feeling the same sensation as before.

"Helena, are you feeling okay?" he asks, moving closer.

"Stay away, Fazza, stay away." I extend my arm, making him stop.

"What's wrong with you? Why are you like this?"

"Like what? Exhausted? Tired of never being heard? Of living in your little world? Fazza, I'm your wife, not your sex object."

My stomach churns, and I run to the bathroom, closing the door behind me and leaning over the toilet as I throw up.

I stay there for a long time until I feel his hand on my hair, holding it back.

"How long have we been married?" His voice is calmer.

"I don't know, it's been five months since I came here, so we must have been married for about three months," I reply, moving away from him.

I get up, go to the sink, turn on the faucet, and wash my face.

"Did you take your injection again? I remember you said it was every three months, and it's been four months now..."

I raise my face, look at my reflection in the mirror, and see Fazza behind me with a serious expression.

Damn, I forgot!

Fazza notices from my expression that I forgot the injection.

"I ask you one thing, not to get pregnant, and what do you do? Get pregnant. *Damn it,* Helena!"

The sheikh walks out of the bathroom, pacing back and forth.

"You almost drive me insane. I've deprived myself of so many things that I forgot the damn injection," I say, following him.

"Why? Why? Why?" He slams his hands on his waist. "I thought we had an agreement!"

"I already told you, I forgot! For.get.ti! — I spell it out for him.

"This is too much for me..."

"Okay, Emir! You made it clear that you don't want a child of ours. Take advantage of the fact that no one knows and give me a divorce. I don't need any of this, I don't need it." My eyes fill with tears again at his refusal of our child.

"Who told you I don't want one? By *Allah*, you drive me crazy, Helena, crazy!"

"ME?" I yell, not understanding.

"Yes, you! You want to know something? Go to Brazil. Go today if you want, but when *Ramadan* is over, I want you back here. Especially now that you're expecting my child."

"You don't know that, I might not even be pregnant," I say, watching him turn his back and leave me alone.

I fall onto my bed and start crying like a small child.

CHAPTER TWENTY-FOUR

Fazza

"Come in, Zaya." I gesture for my first wife to enter the room. I watch Zaya walk into the room, her hijab covering her hair, and I find myself analyzing her expression.

I don't remember the last time I took her to bed.

When I have Helena by my side, I don't care about anything else. This woman has the power to bring out the best in me and make me forget the world when she's in my arms.

"Fazza," Zaya calls me.

I cross my arms, watching her walk around the room, as if she's nervous.

"What is it, Zaya? Is something bothering you?"

"I want a divorce. We always made it clear that if I wanted one, I could just ask, and now I do. I no longer feel comfortable, and I know I'm leaving my daughters in good hands."

I am left speechless.

Not this now?

"Is there a specific reason?" I ask, frowning.

"You know I've always had my disagreements with your family. They don't accept me well, and after Samira arrived, things only got worse. But now with Helena, I feel she will take good care of our daughters."

Even her?

Zaya likes Helena.

It seems everyone likes Helena and judges me for treating her coldly whenever we're with the other wives.

My brothers, Nain, Isa, my daughters, and even Zaya.

Everyone likes her.

I guess this role doesn't extend only to my mother, Samira, and Omar, who insists on saying that Helena is a curse to this Emirate.

"I promised your father that I would leave you to your own decisions. Are you sure about this, Zaya?" I ask, seeing her nod. "Helena will travel to Brazil. Wait for Ramadan, reflect on your decisions, and if after that you still want the divorce, I'll give it to you."

"Alright, fine, Fazza."

I GENTLY PUSH THE DOOR open and see my second wife lying on the bed with our daughter in her arms.

So small and innocent, my newest princess.

I am crazy about my daughters; I don't care that they are girls. My desire for a son is to carry my bloodline forward with my own flesh and blood.

Samira sees me enter while my mother is sitting in an armchair beside her.

"Hello, my sheikh," she says softly.

I sit on the bed and study her sad expression. I raise my hand to smooth her cheek.

"I don't want to see you sad," I murmur.

"I didn't give you our son. It was my role to do so, and I failed."

"Samira, you know this isn't something we can decide. Maybe this isn't Allah's will." I look at our little one with her black, voluminous hair.

"As soon as I'm allowed, I want to try again, sheikh."

I raise my eyes and exhale heavily.

"You won't be able to, Samira. Not if Helena is pregnant," I murmur, recalling that she missed the damned injection.

"What?" Mom rises, approaching. "That Western woman is pregnant?"

I hear Samira sniffle.

"No, no, no! She can't be pregnant. She can't give you our son!"

My wife starts to lose control; I've never seen her in this state before. Perhaps she's become too obsessed with giving me a son.

"Samira, it's a baby. A baby that might be growing inside her, and if it's confirmed, she won't be able to get pregnant again while she's pregnant. That's it, and there's no more room for discussion." I get up from the bed.

My day is already a total torment, and my head feels like it's going to explode.

It was supposed to be a joyful moment; my daughter was born healthy, but everyone is making a fuss.

"And if this obsession with a son doesn't stop, I'll appoint someone else to take my place if something happens to me. Stop this obsession!"

I turn my back, tired of all this shit.

I STAND IN FRONT OF the window in my room, the dark night making me reflective, which is why I chose to retire early.

I hear the sound of the door opening and don't look back, knowing it's Helena coming in. The scent of her perfume is unmistakable.

"Did you call for me, sheikh?"

Her voice is like a melody that fills my ears.

I turn my body; the room is dimly lit by the bedside lamp.

"I did. If you're really going to travel, I want you here with me tonight."

Helena stands there for a moment, and I observe the hijab covering her brown hair.

So beautiful...

The most beautiful features I've ever seen.

She bites her lip in an internal struggle, trying to refuse coming to me. So I walk over to her, dragging my feet on the floor.

"I thought you were angry with me," she murmurs when I stop in front of her.

"I'm crazy about you, Helena. When it comes to you, I go to extremes in seconds."

I remove the hijab, and her long hair falls over her shoulders. I take a strand and bring it to my nose, inhaling its scent.

"Will you let me go?"

I lift her chin, caressing it with my finger, and lose myself in the green of her irises.

"I will, but I need you to take care of yourself. I can't lose you," I say as if it were a necessity.

I push her hair to the side, leaving her neck exposed, and kiss her delicate skin, feeling its softness on my lips.

I move upward until my lips touch hers, initiating a slow kiss.

I feel her tongue against mine and become dizzy, needing more.

I run my hand down her back, pulling down her tunic over her arms until the fabric falls to the floor. I remove her bra, leaving only her panties.

I lift my wife into my arms, carrying her to my bed and laying her on the sheets.

"Fazza." She holds my face, caressing my beard.

I lower my face and give her a brief peck on the lips.

"We can't have sex, not if you're pregnant," I murmur, caressing her waist.

"Please, I want to. It won't harm the baby."

"Helena, you make me break all our customs. I can't be intimate with you if you're pregnant."

"And if I persuade you?"

Quickly, she pushes me, sitting on my lap and grinding against my member, rubbing her panties over the fabric of my pajamas.

I try to control myself, but how can I when I started?

I see her perfect breasts, bare before me.

I raise my hand, pinching the tip of her nipple while Helena pulls down my pants just enough to free my cock.

With her panties to the side, she sits on it, and I close my eyes, feeling her warm, open walls taking me completely.

"Fuck, Helena..." I let slip as she begins to grind.

With several back-and-forth movements, she grinds so deliciously it drives me insane.

I hold her waist, lowering my hand and squeezing her ass tightly.

"Oh, my sheikh, my sheikh..."

Helena bites her lips, causing me to pull her closer, bringing her lips to mine.

I kiss her mouth fiercely, with desire, wanting everything from her.

I moan as she intensifies her movements. Our bodies collide as Helena grinds like a purring cat.

I suck on her tongue and know she is completely surrendered to me.

I feel her walls tightening, and I come deeply, surrendering myself to this woman.

My wife collapses on top of me, our bodies exhausted.

We lie like that for long seconds, as if neither of us wanted to lose contact.

"Please, Helena, come back to me. If you don't return after Ramadan, I'll come to you and bring you back," I say, watching her lift her face from my chest.

Her hair is sweaty, and a relaxed smile is on her lips.

"I will come back; I always do, and I hate myself for it. I hate myself for loving you so much. I hate how alive I feel in your arms. And I hate myself even more for feeling so much pleasure with you. I know I'll hate you when I have to go to bed with one of your other wives..."

Shit, I don't want to lose her!

For Allah, what do I need to do to have her just for myself, body and soul, with no barriers?

CHAPTER TWENTY-FIVE

Helena

I **didn't think** that being away from Fazza would make me miss him so much.

I've been at my mother's house for three weeks, and Fazza hardly calls. Due to Ramadan, he spends most of his time with his family, praying, fasting, and the few times he calls, his voice is calm, and he barely says anything.

I still haven't figured out what to do about the pregnancy because I'm trying to hide it from my family at all costs. I don't want them to suffer knowing that I'm pregnant and in another country.

I tie my hair up in a bun.

I open the door to my old room and step out, smelling the aroma of food in the air. This is something that never happens at the palace; they are against food smells in the environment.

I walk through the living room and see my sister lying on her boyfriend's lap.

In the reflection, I notice that I'm not wearing my hijab and a man is present, but I soon realize I'm not in Agu Dhami and don't need to cover up.

"What's wrong, sister?" Fernanda notices my confusion.

"Nothing, it's just strange. I always wear a hijab when there's a man around, and I was feeling a bit confused," I murmur, frowning.

"You look like a Muslim," my sister says jokingly.

But it hits me hard.

Am I slowly becoming one of them?

It's as if my subconscious is already Muslim. I'm gradually adapting to them; I can't even wear shorts here without feeling like I'm betraying my husband, my "religion," though it reminds me that I haven't converted to Islam.

These days with my family are making me realize that perhaps I am a Muslim and that I'm adopting their culture as if I was born for it.

I'm ready to convert to Islam and teach our child how great this religion is.

I'm pulled out of my reverie when I hear my phone ring. I take it out of my pocket and see Fazza's photo, requesting a video call.

I accept and sit on the sofa facing my sister and her boyfriend.

I can't contain my smile when he appears on the screen.

"Hello, my princess."

His voice is calm, and his beard looks a bit longer.

"How are you, Emir?" I ask, seeing him lying on his bed, holding the phone above his head, with his other arm under his head.

"I'm well, feeling as light as a feather." He gives one of his best smiles.

I get up from the sofa, go to my room, and close the door behind me.

"Has Ramadan ended?"

"Yes, two days ago. When are you coming back?"

I don't respond and lie down on the bed.

Staying in Brazil has been nice, but I barely go outside, especially since it was discovered that the princess of sheikh Fazza was in the country. They even wanted to hold a press conference, but I refused all of them in the first week. The journalists camped out at my family's apartment entrance until they gave up when they realized I wouldn't say a word.

Nain helped me stay silent because now that I'm part of the royal family, anything could be used against me.

"Helena? You're not going to make me leave Agu Dhami, are you?"
I smile seeing his serious expression.
"No, my sheikh, I'll be back. How are things there?"
"Calm, I think..." Fazza furrows his brow, making me smile.
Soon, I think of Samira, now she's free to warm his bed.
"Fazza, can I ask you a question?"
"Here you go with your difficult questions." My husband closes his eyes, signaling for me to continue.
"Have you been with any of your two wives in the past two days?"
He says nothing, not even opening his eyes. I feel my stomach churn with the sensation of him going to be with one of them.
"No," he finally answers, opening his eyes "but it's complicated, Helena. I have to honor my role as a husband. Zaya doesn't mind, but Samira has shown signs of discontent."
"But you can't get either of them pregnant if I'm pregnant," I murmur, being selfish.
"Yes, but what about desire? Did you lie with me to get me pregnant?"
"Our case is different," I murmur.
"I don't know what to do, I don't know, Helena. I want you more than anything in this life, but it doesn't work this way. I need to honor my role as a man..."
Tears fill my eyes, and not wanting to talk to him anymore, I end the call without saying goodbye or even a word.
Tears roll down my face.
How can I love someone who isn't only mine?
My phone rings again, but this time I don't answer.
I'm startled to see my sister enter my room.
"Oh, heavens! You're crying, Helena."
"Please, answer the phone and tell Fazza that I'll be back tomorrow and that I don't want to talk to him right now," I ask my sister.

Fernanda doesn't question it, answers the phone, but instead of saying what I asked, she starts cursing my husband.

"You asshole, you've ruined my sister! If it were up to me, she'd never go back to that Emirate. Meeting you was the worst thing that could happen to Helena's life. She said to let you know that she's coming back tomorrow to this place you call home."

Fernanda doesn't give him a chance to speak and quickly hangs up.

She sits next to me, pulling me into her arms.

"Helena, please don't go back," she pleads, smelling my hair.

"I can't, I wish it were that simple," I murmur, sniffling.

"Why isn't it simple? Helena, what's behind all this love you have for this man?"

I begin to talk about our contract, especially, making it clear that I sold myself to him without even realizing it, and finally say:

"And it seems that I'm pregnant. Pregnant with the sheikh's child," I say with tear-streaked eyes.

"Pregnant? For God's sake, Helena." My sister hugs me tightly. "You're going back to that Emirate and sending me a copy of the contract. I'll find a way to get you out of this situation. No matter how much you love this sheikh, you weren't born to be shared in a man's heart. You were born to be the only one, sister."

CHAPTER TWENTY-SIX

Fazza

I observe everyone present in the room, and Zaya looks at me as if she's waiting for me to take the necessary action.

I sigh.

I don't want to break the agreement I made with her father.

I waited until the end of Ramadan, even considered backing out, but Zaya is determined.

"Family," I finally say, drawing everyone's attention. "Given certain circumstances, Zaya no longer feels comfortable among us. It wasn't easy for me, but with everyone here as witnesses..." I stop speaking and rise from the armchair with Zaya following me. "I repudiate you, I repudiate you." I close my eyes.

Even though we didn't have an intimate bond, this divorce is painful.

I open my eyes and everyone looks at me in astonishment; no one expected this.

"I repudiate you, Zaya," I say loudly, repeating the three "I repudiate yous," thus making our divorce official with everyone as witnesses.

"Thank you, sheikh," Zaya says in a whisper.

I raise my eyes toward the door and see Helena passing by.

I never thought I'd miss someone as much as I miss her.

My wife enters the room, and all eyes turn to her.

"I guess I came at a bad time," she says with a half-smile.

"I'm glad to see you before leaving the palace, Helena," Zaya says loudly.

"Oh, no, Zaya."

From Helena's expression, it's clear she knew about Zaya's request, which is not surprising, since the two were always whispering to each other.

"HELENA" Safira runs into the room, shouting upon seeing my wife.

Safira hugs Helena around the waist, and like me, everyone watches the two of them embrace.

"Oh, my little one." Helena kisses the top of Safira's head and whispers something, making my daughter break into a wide smile.

"Safira, don't forget that your mother is someone else," my mother says. "Be polite."

"She didn't do anything wrong, Mom." I return to my armchair.

"We know it's not good for the children to be around her; she isn't even Muslim. What example can she set for them?" My mother insists.

The whole room falls silent, and I close my eyes briefly.

"That's exactly what I want to talk to the emir about," Helena says, drawing my attention.

I open my eyes, staring at her delicate face.

She keeps her gaze fixed on mine while hugging my daughter's waist.

"What do you mean, Helena?" I ask, scratching my beard.

"I'll explain when we're alone. For now, I want to catch up with this little one."

I can't help but smile seeing Helena's connection with my daughters.

"Don't forget that if you're pregnant, you can't sleep with the emir." Mom resumes her venomous remarks.

"I haven't forgotten, mother-in-law." Helena smiles at my mother in a somewhat forced gesture. "But since I'm not sure yet, for all intents and purposes, I'm not pregnant."

"What do you mean?" my mother asks, somewhat agitated.

"Enough, Mom. I know my duties as a man; you don't need to keep reminding me. — I rise from the armchair, feeling exhausted by the topic. — Helena is my wife, just like Samira, and I demand respect." I turn my back. "Come with me, Helena. Safira, you can talk to her later." I gesture for my wife to follow me.

"Where are we going?" Helena asks curiously as we exit the palace through the back door.

I want to grab her, take her to a corner, devour her lips, and keep her in my bed until we're both satisfied.

"I'm going to introduce you to my animals, Ali and Aziz."

"Oh, no, thank you, I don't want to."

I smile as I see the woman turning around, wanting to leave, but I'm faster and grab her hand.

"Unfortunately, I didn't give you that option." I smile, pulling her arm.

"Fazza, can't it be a dog? Does it have to be a lion?"

"Maybe it's not what you're thinking."

Helena huffs and rolls her eyes.

"What a lovely reception, seeing a lion. Is today the day I become feline food?"

"So much drama!" I can't help but smile.

"Of course, it's totally normal, a lion as a pet."

"By the way, I've missed you so much," I murmur, seeing a sparkle form in her eyes.

"I'm noticing. Is that why you're going to throw me into the lion's den?"

"Actually, it's a lion and a lioness." I wink.

I intertwine my fingers with Helena's and we walk down the corridor, where a double door opens for us.

The door is closed as soon as we pass through.

I see my lions sitting next to a sofa. This side of the palace is what I call my fun side.

I have a few cars, my felines stay here, and a room if I want to sleep on this side.

"Shit, Fazza, they're real." My wife hides behind me when she sees the two getting up.

Aziz is the first to come towards me; my white lion has a smooth and graceful gait.

I let the lion approach, and as it gets close, it lowers its head, asking for attention.

"See?." I pet its silky fur.

The feline sits in front of me.

"Aziz, buddy, this is Helena." I hold my wife's hand.

With great effort, I make the lion sniff her hand, letting it recognize her.

"Damn, this is crazy!" my wife whispers as she watches my lion sniff her hand.

Soon, Ali, my lioness, joins us, and both demand attention. I release Helena's hand and kneel while the two sniff my face.

"Fazza, for heaven's sake, this is too much craziness," Helena says, terrified, making me laugh.

"They don't do anything, at least not to me. It's who they respect. Come on?" I extend my hand, and with great reluctance, she sits on the floor.

Aziz rests his head on her lap.

My wife is slightly terrified but soon starts to pet his head.

I watch the scene.

"Did you give Zaya the divorce?" she asks in a whisper.

"I did, but I don't want to talk about it, not now..."

I take my phone, open the camera, and take a picture of her with Aziz, a moment of relaxation.

"Can I post it?" I ask.

"On your social media?"

I nod.

"But you hardly ever post anything there."

"Precisely, isn't there better content than my wife with my baby?" I smile, watching her lift her head.

"It's a rather large baby, don't you think?" she murmurs.

"I didn't specify which baby."

Her eyes lift from the feline to me.

This month away from her made me realize I want this baby with her.

I didn't have a clear vision of Samira wanting to join me in bed, and now that Ramadan is over and she's available, as a husband, I need to take her to my sheets.

But there's Helena, and I don't want to disappoint her.

I believe there's no better solution for this.

"My sheikh..."

I snap out of my thoughts when Helena calls me with her soft voice and turn to look into her beautiful, shining green eyes.

"Yes, my princess."

"This time away made me realize that I'm ready to convert to Islam. I want to be able to teach our child about this wonderful culture that I am passionate about and have inadvertently adopted for myself."

I raise my hand, caressing her face, taking advantage of the fact that no one is close by.

"It's what I desire most, Helena. I didn't want to cross your boundaries by imposing this on you, as I believe this choice must come from your heart. I confess I'm overjoyed with your decision." I wink, watching her become embarrassed and lower her face, petting my lion.

CHAPTER TWENTY-SEVEN

Helena

I look through the window of my room at the dark night while sighing in frustration.

Fazza hasn't called me to his room, and I don't even know if he's home.

My arrival at the palace wasn't received with much joy, which is no surprise, and my husband is somewhat distant, especially now with the divorce from Zaya.

I exhale forcefully, grab my hijab from the bed, and cover my hair. I leave the room, finding everything in perfect silence.

"What are you doing walking around alone at this hour?"

I startle when I look back and see Samira.

"I think I could ask you the same question," I murmur.

"I'm going to the sheikh's room, and you?"

I swallow hard, as this is not what I was expecting; it feels like I've been punched in the stomach.

Samira has a victorious smile on her lips.

"I'm just walking around," I say, lifting my head.

"You should stay in your room; this isn't a tourist attraction."

"Wait." I raise my finger as if I'm thinking. "Did I ask for your opinion? Oh, no!" I smile at her mockingly.

"Now that Zaya is leaving, it will be even easier to send you away and be the only wife. The sheikh will get tired of you soon enough."

"I wish I had your self-esteem." I close the distance between us, and I can see Samira swallow hard.

Her gaze falls on my back; I follow her gaze and see Fazza approaching.

I turn my body and narrow my eyes towards my husband.

"May I know what's going on here?" His voice is deep.

"Nothing, my sheikh. I'm just telling Helena that she shouldn't be wandering the hallway alone."

I turn my face towards Samira at her sweet voice.

"Funny, I don't see you accompanied by anyone," he says, and I cross my arms.

"I was coming from our daughter's room." He smiles, changing what she had told me earlier.

"Samira." We both look towards Fazza. "Go to your room, please."

She even tries to clear her throat but is not crazy enough to go against a sheikh's order.

I turn my back to him, about to head to my room when I feel his fingers grip my wrist.

"You're coming with me," he murmurs as soon as we're alone.

"I thought that..." I turn my neck towards him.

"You're thinking too much, come on!"

Fazza holds my hand, and we head to his room.

My husband opens the door for me to enter first. Once inside, I see that it's still the same, cozy and large.

"I thought you had called Samira," I say as soon as we're alone.

"No, I just came back from the mosque. I was on my way to call you." He holds my hand.

I lift my face towards him, how I've missed him.

I'd rather not mention that Samira lied and enjoy the moment.

"A bath with me?" he asks, holding my waist.

"I've already taken a bath," I murmur, unable to resist my smile.

"One more or one less..."

Fazza pulls me close, his body pressed against mine, his face lowering to plant kisses on my neck, and I can't help but sigh.

"A doctor is coming tomorrow," he says close to my skin.

"I feel like if I'm pregnant, you'll pull away, and even though I know I am, I don't want to admit it. I don't want to be in a separate room, Fazza." I lift my eyes to his.

He raises his hand, caressing my face, and I instinctively close my eyes as his lips meet mine in a slow, calm kiss.

"I missed you," he murmurs again.

"I missed you too, my sheikh."

We smile against each other's lips.

His hand intertwines with mine as we walk towards the bathroom.

Fazza removes my tunic, pulling it over my head, leaving me in just my underwear. The hijab falls to the floor along with the tunic.

I help my husband remove his tunic and caress his chest, which has only a few hairs. I bring my lips close, placing scattered kisses, and hold the waistband of his underwear, pulling it down his toned legs.

The sheikh holds my hair when he sees I'm bending down.

"Helena..."

I straighten up, easily remove my bra and panties, and he picks me up in his arms.

"So beautiful..." he murmurs, kissing my neck.

He turns on the shower, and soon the water falls over us.

"I can't stand being away from you for so long. Away from your scent, your smile."

His cock nudges me between my legs.

"We can't do it, but I can't take it anymore," Fazza growls in his deep voice.

"Please, husband, I want it. I want you to fuck me hard, it won't hurt me."

I feel my back pressed against the cold wall as I grind against his erect member.

I'm almost begging for him to penetrate me forcefully.

"Fazza," I plead in a desperate tone.

I run my hand through his wet hair, and with much reluctance, he penetrates me.

"Fuck, I've missed this pussy so much."

He goes all the way in, moving slowly with the water running down his back.

My nails scratch his skin as I let out small moans.

The sheikh takes my mouth with lust.

In a slow rhythm, our tongues dance, his beard brushes against my face, and I can't control myself, moaning on his arm.

My legs are wrapped around his waist, and his broad chest presses against mine. His hand moves to my neck and grips my hair.

"Helena," he murmurs between kisses. "Mine, only mine..."

His voice carries a possessive tone, as if I were his sole property. And at this point, I guess I am this man's.

How could I not be when my heart already belongs to him, even if I didn't want it to?

Fazza starts intensifying the movements, thrusting hard with our bodies colliding.

I give in and let the orgasm take over, my walls contracting around his cock.

The sheikh doesn't take long and soon reaches his release along with me.

We stay like this for long seconds, only the sound of water hitting the floor and our accelerated breathing echoing in the room.

How I've missed him, his body, the way his beard brushes against my skin, and the pleasurable sensation Fazza brings me.

CHAPTER TWENTY-EIGHT

Helena

I **leave** my room adjusting my hijab and find no one in my path. I descend the stairs, hearing voices coming from the breakfast table, and enter the room.

Fazza is already seated at the end of the table.

A servant pulls out a chair for me to sit in, and I take my seat.

"Helena." I lift my face toward my mother-in-law. "I want to be present at my grandson's appointment."

I open my mouth several times; Aiyra has never bothered to stay in the same room as me, so this is unusual.

"Okay, fine," I finally murmur.

I glance to the side, and Fazza has a smile on his lips, as if mocking my reaction.

"Mother-in-law, can we go to the mall later?" Samira draws Aiyra's attention.

"Better not, Samira, even though the doctor has cleared you, it's still too early to leave Aysha alone."

I bite my lip, holding back a smile.

Did I wake up in the right house?

What the *hell* is going on around here?

What did I miss?

Samira says nothing.

My eyes catch sight of Layla entering the room like a *little whirlwind*.

"Layla, manners," the grandmother reprimands her granddaughter.

"Sorry, grandma. Helena, let's go to my room; I want to show you a new dance routine I learned," the little girl says excitedly, stopping by my side.

"And you're going to teach me?" I ask, unable to contain my smile at seeing her eyes light up.

"YES!" she screams, clapping her hands. "I'm a great teacher and one day I'll be a good wife."

I hold her face, caressing her cheek and kissing her forehead.

"I'll come by later." I wink.

"Helena, don't forget that you're pregnant, you shouldn't overexert yourself." I look toward Aiyra.

"Mother-in-law, pregnancy isn't synonymous with illness."

"THAT'S RIGHT!" Layla screams again, making me look at her with a grimace. "Especially since it's twins."

The whole room falls silent.

"I dreamed that I was going to have two twin siblings," the girl speaks again, breaking the silence.

"Good thing it was just a dream," I say.

"Layla predicted Samira's and her mother's pregnancies correctly," Aiyra says with an excited voice.

"Please, no expectations," I murmur, closing my eyes with a shiver.

I don't want to witness the same expectations they had with Samira.

Layla rushes out of the room.

I eat very little, lacking appetite, especially after this twin story.

"I have unavoidable commitments today; if you need anything, message me, Helena," Fazza says, getting up from the table.

I can't help but notice his light blue jeans with a button-down shirt tucked into them, highlighting his well-defined legs in the jeans.

I swallow hard.

He notices my quick appraisal and gives a sideways smile.

"I will," I finally reply.

Fazza bids everyone farewell with a brief nod of his head, accompanied by his brother Khalil.

"HERE," AIYRA OPENS a door.

Accompanied by my mother-in-law, I enter what seems to be a consultation room.

Why am I still surprised?

They have an office inside this enormous palace.

"Hello, Princess Al-Sabbah." The woman stands up from her chair with a brief nod. "It's a pleasure to see you again, Sheikha Aiyra."

We sit in front of the doctor's desk.

"Do you remember when your last period was?" She gets straight to the point.

"No, actually, I didn't even get it. I was using the quarterly injection and forgot to take the new dose. Well, I think I'm pregnant."

She asks a few more questions, wanting to know the date I took the injection.

"Haven't you done any tests?"

"No."

"Given the time you mentioned, if you're pregnant, it's already an advanced pregnancy, which is a mistake. You should have contacted me sooner."

After the scolding, she asks me to lie down on the examination table.

I get up from the chair with my mother-in-law always by my side.

Fortunately, today I chose to wear *cirwal*, the pants worn under the tunic, so I can lift it without embarrassment with my mother-in-law beside me.

The doctor positions herself, turns on all the machines, and applies gel to my belly, which feels cold.

I get a brief scare when I feel Aiyra's hand holding my fingers.

Is all this because of the pregnancy?

I lift my face as I see the woman rubbing the device on my belly and blurs appearing on the screen.

"Here..." She points with the mouse. "As expected, you're about thirteen weeks along."

"So, doctor, is everything okay with my grandson?" Aiyra asks, worried.

"Yes, everything is within normal limits. Excuse me" she says, adjusting the device on my belly. "See, here are the little legs, the arms, but there's something confusing me. I'll move the device more on your belly and see if the baby moves. Cough, Helena."

I pretend to cough, doing as the doctor asks.

"Why, doctor? Didn't you ask my other daughters-in-law to do this?" Aiyra asks, looking from the screen to my belly.

I see on the screen my baby moving and feel my eyes welling up with tears.

How can something like this be growing inside me?

Little legs, arms, and I don't even have a belly yet.

"Everything is fine, Sheikha. As I predicted, here..." She shows on the screen. "There was someone hiding behind the other baby; now both are awake. They are twins, congratulations. They seem to be healthy, but since it's a twin pregnancy, we'll need to double the care."

"Twins?" I ask, recalling Layla's words.

My mother-in-law releases my hand, covering her mouth reflexively.

"Our prayers have been heard," Aiyra holds back her tears. "Thank you, Helena. By Allah, only I know how much I prayed for my son."

She takes my hand again, as if I were something fragile, looking at me with such devotion.

"Do you want to hear the heartbeats?"

"Is that possible?" I ask, letting the tears overflow from my eyes.

The doctor smiles, making the sound echo in the room. Like a samba school, the two little hearts growing in my womb beat irregularly.

I take out my phone, open the conversation with Fazza, and record the sound of our babies' heartbeat.

He immediately views the message and I type through my tears.

"Congratulations, Daddy, *we're having twins*"

What is this fate?

I never thought I would have a child by a sheikh, and now I'm expecting twins from the Emir of Agu Dhami.

CHAPTER TWENTY-NINE

Helena

The music plays in the room, and everyone dances with enthusiasm.

I can't help but smile as I see Safira pulling her father by the hand to join the others.

The palace is filled with immense joy; they don't even know the gender of my babies yet, but given Layla's dream, everyone is already convinced that my babies are two boys.

Khalil, my brother-in-law, sees me alone and comes over.

"Come on, sister-in-law, today is a day of joy." He practically pushes me towards the others.

Among all of Fazza's siblings, Khalil is the only one I talk to occasionally.

Khalil runs his hand through his hair, pushing it back. His eyes have a dark green hue and he looks nothing like Fazza; it must be because they have different mothers.

I can't contain my laughter when I see Khalil pulling Layla, watching her dance with us. The girl raises her hand, making the jewel on her wrist sparkle.

I am amazed at how these girls already have such clear ideas about what they want from life.

I glance to the side and my eyes meet my husband's. He has a beautiful smile on his lips, which I want to kiss and feel his beard on my skin.

Discreetly, he winks as if he's reading my thoughts or even thinking the same thing.

Although I'm enjoying the joy, I feel exhausted and tired.

The day has been full; there was Zaya's farewell, and her daughters cried a lot, but in the end, they understood.

I promised Zaya that I would take care of Safira, Layla, and Jamile as if they were my own daughters, and I will.

Their divorce was amicable, and Fazza even seems a bit relieved, as if he's granting freedom to his wife.

I move away from them, spotting my mother-in-law who gestures for me to come closer.

I walk towards her, watching her stop dancing.

"How are you feeling, dear?"

"A bit tired; I think I'm going to head out," I say, searching for Fazza with my eyes.

"If you want, I can have the music turned down. Nothing should interfere with the mother of my grandchildren." She shakes her head briefly with a smile on her lips.

I admit this kind side of my mother-in-law makes me uneasy.

All this because of a pregnancy?

"Don't take it the wrong way, but why, Aiyra?" I ask, frowning.

"I don't understand?"

"Why this sudden change?"

"Ramadan made me reflect on all my actions and how I was being unfair to you without even giving you a chance. I always strive for the best for my children, and sometimes, out of my own selfishness, I end up acting wrongly."

I follow my mother-in-law's gaze and we witness Samira coming down the stairs towards Fazza.

"The walls of this palace will still shake. May Allah watch over us! I feel in my heart that Fazza won't be able to maintain one of his marriages; I've never seen my son like this..."

Aiyra lets the sentence trail off as Samira fixes her gaze on us. She changes her course, coming towards the two of us.

"Didn't you say you were tired? Now is the best time to leave, Helena," Aiyra says before Samira approaches.

I agree with her; I'm not in the best condition to argue with Samira, not after this tumultuous day when all I want is to end up in bed with my husband.

With a brief nod, I bid farewell to my mother-in-law.

I reach the stairs and look back, needing to see where Fazza is. Like an invisible connection, he looks at me at the same moment.

I smile with relief as I see him saying goodbye to some people and coming towards me.

I begin to ascend step by step, and when I reach the top, I can hear his steps very close behind me.

"To my room, princess?"

His voice is a whisper close to my ear.

"Is that an order?" I ask, glancing over my shoulder.

"As if you obey all my wishes."

I can't help but smile.

"Finally, some sensible words."

I bite the corner of my mouth, turning down the hallway toward his room.

I let out a laugh when he embraces me from behind.

"Fazza, someone might see us," I say as he lifts me into his arms.

"They're all downstairs."

His black eyes meet mine, and there's a bright gleam in them.

I slide my hand around his back, and he pushes open the door to his room with his free hand.

"I can't have you while you're pregnant, but I'm selfish and I want you anyway, even if it's just to sleep by my side. Your presence warms my heart." His voice is a whisper.

The door closes behind us, and my husband moves toward the bed, laying me down on the white sheets.

"So let me stay here with you," I murmur, holding onto his tunic to keep him close.

"It's all so complicated..." Fazza rests his knee on the bed.

I close my eyes as I feel his hand caress my face.

"Simplify it, my sheikh," I whisper softly.

"I love it when you call me your sheikh..."

"I wish you were entirely mine." I open my eyes.

We stare at each other for long minutes.

"How far would you go for me, Fazza?" I ask boldly. "What's the depth of your feelings for me, Fazza?" I bite the corner of my lips, afraid of his answer.

I close my eyes as I see him get up, avoiding my question.

Soon the bed sinks beside me, and I open my eyes again. I see Fazza raising his arm and placing his hand on my belly, as if he's claiming our children too.

"I can't answer that question because I don't have an answer. If I tell you I love you right now, I might be lying. Honestly, I don't know; feelings have never been expected of me, so I don't know how to gauge what's inside me."

I prefer to turn my face to the wall, away from him.

How foolish I was!

Fazza wouldn't go anywhere for me; I'm nothing more than carnal desire, and I'm still the same as at the beginning of our marriage in his eyes—nothing has changed. I even thought I had changed, that he might at least want only me.

I remove his hand from my belly and sit up on the bed.

"I'm going to my room; we need to remember that this is still a contract. You've just made it very clear that you want me only for my body..." I huff without looking at him.

His words hurt me.

How could I think anything had changed?

"Helena..." He is quicker and grabs my hand when I try to get up. "I don't have the answer to your question right now, but I promise I'll think about it."

I turn my face away, forcing a smile.

"If you're going to think about it, it means you don't know. I'm not going to demand anything, Fazza; after all, there's nothing to demand. From the beginning, I knew you had other women. Maybe it's time to face reality. Sooner or later, you'll have to lie down with her, and I'd rather that happen as soon as possible so I can remove this love I feel for you from inside me."

The tears I've held back begin to flow down my face.

I pull my hand away forcefully and leave the room, practically running. I need to stay away from him, tormenting myself with the lies I've told.

I don't want him with another.

I want Fazza with me, only with me!

CHAPTER THIRTY

Helena

"Helena." I hear a child's voice calling me and open my eyes, blinking a few times.

"What are you doing here?" Safira asks, her face close to mine.

I smile shyly.

Last night, I didn't want to be alone in my room and feeling lonely, I came to the girls' room.

"I couldn't sleep, so I came to see the most beautiful girls and ended up falling asleep," I murmur, sitting up on the bed.

Layla, who was still sleeping, wakes up with our conversation.

"Mommy?" the girl says sleepily.

"It's Helena; she came to stay with us," Safira says happily.

Soon the nannies join us in the room, and I leave, walking down the corridor toward my room.

As I walk, I hear whispers and slow down to listen better, distinguishing the voices.

Fazza is talking to Samira.

Is it wrong of me to overhear their conversation?

But my curious side gets the better of me, and I hear everything.

"Samira, please..."

I have to take a few more steps to hear better, as Fazza lowers his voice.

"Fazza, I want it!"

From Samira's tone, it's clear she's irritated.

"Alright, tonight, in my room. Be there and don't tell anyone. I don't want rumors spreading through the palace walls..."

My heart skips a beat, and I turn around, wanting to run and hide again.

Taking a longer route, I reach my room, lock the door, and run my hand over my face, holding back my tears.

I need to be strong, I need to think!

I walk to my bed and grab my phone from the pillow.

I unlock the screen and see a message from Fernanda asking how I'm doing.

I immediately place my hand on my belly, wanting to protect my children, to shield them from the madness of seeing their father divided among several women.

My chest hurts and anxiety overwhelms me.

My eyes fix on a suitcase, and soon an idea comes to mind.

Is running away the best choice?

Fazza will be busy in Samira's arms.

Thinking about it makes me grimace with disgust.

I know it's pointless to run; the sheikh will find me wherever I go, but right now my rational side isn't working, and all I want is to be with my family.

THE HOUSE IS IN COMPLETE silence; I'm wearing jeans, a shirt, and a robe over it just to leave the palace unnoticed.

The advantage of wearing the hijab is that when I leave the palace, I can take it off and no one will recognize me, at least not here in the Emirates.

I haven't seen Fazza today; perhaps it's because I spent the entire day in my room. My task of avoiding him was successful.

Deep down, I wanted to see him, maybe just one last time, to make sure I'm making the right decision.

I check my phone and realize it's time to put my plan into action. If everything goes as expected, I believe they'll only notice my absence the following morning, and I won't have even reached Brazil yet.

I huff in frustration.

I grab my hijab from the bed and leave the room. I can't think any longer; I need to act. I can't bear to wake up the next morning and see him knowing he slept with Samira.

I walk with my head down; I can't take any luggage, or it will be too obvious that I'm running away.

"Helena."

I look back and see Safira with tears in her eyes.

"Where are you going?"

The little girl, just seven years old, holds Jamile, who is fussing non-stop, in her lap.

I walk over to them and take the baby into my arms.

"What's wrong, my angel?" I ask, soothing the baby and calming her down.

"Jamile was whining, and we couldn't call the nanny, so we came to find you."

I can't help but smile.

How can I not fall in love with these three girls?

"Why don't we all lie down in my room?" I suggest, remembering that this is another night I'm spending away from my husband.

I wonder what he's doing now.

I enter my room with the girls, watching my escape plan go down the drain.

Safira and Layla run to the bed and lie down while I follow with little Jamile.

I NEED TO FACE REALITY and have breakfast with the family.

I leave the girls in their room, where the nannies look at me in alarm. I explain what happened, and they smile with relief when they realize I took care of the girls.

I spend a little while helping to change little Jamile.

It's no sacrifice for me to be with them.

When I see there's no escape, I gather all my dignity and leave the girls' room. I walk down the hallway, go down the stairs, and hear voices coming from the breakfast room.

I try to be quiet as I enter the room, but my attempt is in vain, as Aiyra sees me and asks:

"Are you feeling better, Helena?"

"I think so," I murmur, looking down.

"I heard the girls went looking for you the night before," my mother-in-law says as I pull a chair farther away from Fazza.

"Yes, they came looking for me and slept in my room," I say, picking up a piece of strawberry from a bowl near me.

"Why did they look for you, Helena? They must have passed by my room and seen that it was empty."

My heart freezes at Samira's words, which she insists on throwing in my face.

I don't say anything, feeling my appetite vanish.

"Helena, dear, you need to eat better. Don't forget that you now have two babies to feed." Aiyra notices that I'm not touching anything.

How can I eat in front of the table where my husband is, who has been with another woman, another who is also his wife?

I can't, I just can't!

I won't be able to look at Fazza and know that he has another wife, that he shares the affection that was supposed to be only mine with her.

My body trembles; I get up from the chair, look at nothing, and say loudly for everyone to hear:

"I want a divorce, I can't take this anymore."

I don't look at Fazza; I don't want to see his reaction.

CHAPTER THIRTY-ONE

Fazza

I **slam** my hand on the table and stand up with everyone around us looking horrified.

"Repeat what you said, Helena, I must be deaf..." My voice comes out deeper than expected.

Helena doesn't even look in my direction, as if she's been avoiding me all along.

She knows that Samira was in my room.

What the hell!

How did she find out?

"I think you understood well," she says in a robotic tone.

Damn it, it wasn't supposed to end like this!

I feel the situation slipping out of control and I hate that feeling.

I hate feeling everything slipping through my fingers.

"Let's go to my office to talk, Helena." I leave the table.

"Why don't you give your wife what she wants, brother?" Omar says with mockery.

I take a deep breath, recalling the words my father always said, "never act out of anger."

"Come on, Helena," I ask, clenching my fist.

"No, Fazza! What you have to do needs a witness," she says.

She must be crazy if she thinks I'm going to grant a divorce, especially while she's pregnant.

"Helena!" I call her again, my voice deep.

She remains unyielding.

How did I let this happen?

Losing the little patience I have left, I walk up to her, grab her arm, and pull her forcefully. I walk through the room dragging my wife by the hand.

"Let me go, I can walk on my own," she says like a spoiled child.

"Funny, that wasn't how it seemed a few minutes ago."

I open the door to my office, make her enter, and lock the door behind us.

"What the hell do you think you're doing?" I ask, getting straight to the point.

"I don't want this anymore, Fazza. I can't do it, I can't," she says without looking at me.

I see her steps heading towards the sofa, holding onto the backrest.

"Helena..." I sigh deeply. "What's going on in your head?" I ask, taking slow steps towards her.

"You still have the audacity to ask? I heard your conversation in the hallway yesterday. I know everything! You went to bed with her and wanted to keep it secret."

Suddenly her face turns towards me and I see hurt, disillusionment, and the sparkle that was there before is gone.

"It's not what you think," I murmur.

"It's what I saw, Fazza. There's no argument against the evidence."

I see a tear roll down her face, a tear of the pain I'm causing.

"Helena, I'm not going to lie. I sent Samira to my room, but..." I can't finish speaking.

Flashes of the previous night come to my mind, Samira lying naked on my bed, and I could have done whatever I wanted with her, but I couldn't. All I wanted at that moment was Helena, I wanted her hair spread on my pillow, her sweet and yet seductive smile.

I didn't even advance beyond a peck on her lips; it's as if my heart spoke louder, stopping me from proceeding.

Like a cowardly dog, I left Samira on my bed and slept in my office. I thought about looking for Helena, but after the argument we had, I gave up.

"But what, Fazza? Are you going to say you didn't go to bed with her?" my wife asks, frowning.

"If I say I didn't, will you believe me?" I ask, taking a few steps and stopping in front of her.

"No, I won't believe you." She wipes her face, drying her tears.

"See, nothing I say will make you believe me. I didn't sleep with Samira, I left her in my room and came to the office. I couldn't bring myself to sleep with her. I know our agreement was solely for pleasure and I didn't give you the answer you wanted, but now I have the answer." I want to hold her hand, but Helena pulls away.

"Maybe now it's too late." She moves away, walking around the room.

"You know it's not too late."

She looks at me over her shoulder.

"I'm not going to give you a divorce, of all the craziness in the world, that's one thing I won't do. Helena, you're mine, understand? Mine!" I walk towards her, but she evades me.

I want this woman with all my strength; I desire her like I've never desired anyone before.

Helena brings out my most controlling, possessive side, and I'll never allow another man to touch her or have any thoughts about my woman.

She is mine, *only mine!*

"I'll ask for a divorce from Samira," I finally say, drawing her attention.

Helena's eyes widen, and a silence fills the air.

"Wasn't that what you wanted? Didn't you want me only for yourself? Now you'll have it," I say somewhat arrogantly.

"Go to hell, Fazza! Divorce her and you'll be alone. I'm not asking for any charity. When I said I wanted you only for myself, it was out of love, not out of your possessive feelings. Not everything in life goes as you want." She gestures with her hand, showing her frustration with the situation.

"I really don't understand you."

"Just get the divorce if that's what you want, what your heart desires. I don't want to be blamed for something you did for me. And also, I've heard there's a fidelity contract..."

"What are you talking about?" I ask, raising an eyebrow.

"There's a fidelity contract where you promise me that you'll never marry another woman. It's either me or you can be with others and leave me free. Now open the *damn* door; I need to breathe..."

Before I lose the last bit of sanity, I open the door and Helena storms out like a hurricane.

I stand there, thinking about her words.

I want her, and there's no doubt about that. As for the contract, I don't care; I just want Helena in my life.

But for that, I'll have to divorce Samira.

CHAPTER THIRTY-TWO

Helena

Raised voices come from downstairs, and I follow the sound, dragging my feet on the floor. I descend the last flight of stairs, looking towards the living room where tempers are flaring.

Samira is crying in Aiyra's arms, who is stroking her hair.

"This is madness, Fazza! Why are you doing this?" my mother-in-law questions with a melancholic voice.

"It's decided, Mom..." He holds onto the back of the sofa.

I keep my distance, watching everything from afar.

"I repudiate you..." Fazza begins to speak but is interrupted by Samira.

"No, no... I refuse to hear this." Samira covers her ears. "I'm waiting for you, Fazza. I'm waiting for you, my sheikh," she pleads through her tears.

What does she mean by "I'm waiting for you"?

Was what he told me earlier in the office true?

"I repudiate you..."

Samira releases herself from Aiyra, goes to Fazza, and throws herself at his feet.

"Please, Fazza, no... For Allah, what will become of me?" Samira clutches at his robe.

I see Fazza closing his eyes, clenching his hand by his side.

"I... Repudiate... You," he says for the third time.

"NOOOOOOOOO!" Samira screams.

The entire palace falls silent, and only the echoes of Samira's crying are heard.

I must admit I feel pity for her.

Suddenly, Samira lifts her face and her eyes come in my direction.

"IT'S ALL YOUR FAULT, YOU..."

The woman stands up, runs towards me, and I am caught off guard. Before I know it, she is pulling at my hijab and grabbing my hair forcefully. I try to evade and defend myself, but I'm at a disadvantage and can't react.

My scalp burns.

Screams are heard, and when I look, men are trying to pull Samira away from me, but she clings so tightly to my hair that she pulls me along.

"YOU VIPER, YOU CAME TO MY PALACE TO RUIN MY LIFE!" Samira screams uncontrollably.

I feel arms around my waist and know it's Fazza; the firm grip could only be his hands.

Thinking quickly, I grip her arm and press my nail into her skin. My grip is so strong that she screams in pain, finally releasing my hair.

Fazza quickly pulls me away, cradling my hair against his chest as if protecting me.

"If you weren't here, everything would be as it was before!" Samira rages, struggling in the arms of whoever is holding her.

I don't pay attention, as Fazza swiftly grabs my hijab, covering my head, and leads me out of the chaos.

I cling to his chest, walking by his side.

"Take me to my room," I ask, feeling powerless.

"No, I'm not leaving you alone."

I don't say anything; I have no strength to argue, I just want a little peace.

I take a deep breath, feeling the smell of my husband invade my senses.

Soon, he opens a door and we enter his room.

"You were faster than I expected," I murmur, releasing him and heading towards the bed.

Fazza huffs.

I don't pay attention to him; I lie down on his bed and close my eyes, feeling his presence in the room.

Soon, I hear the sound of the door closing and the shower being turned on. It's quite typical of him to take a shower to clear his thoughts.

I lie on my side, and images of him in the shower come to my mind. His broad chest, the few hairs on his tanned skin, the beard framing his face, wet with droplets of water.

I moisten my lips as I remember his long legs and how the water must be cascading down them.

Even though I'm on the verge of giving in to him, I need to be strong and resilient.

I won't surrender to Fazza.

At least I'll try.

I hear the sound of the shower turning off, and I quickly sit up in bed, look around, and grab my hijab. I stand up, heading towards the door, and with one last sigh, I leave the room.

I don't trust myself when I'm near him.

I told Fazza I wouldn't give myself to him just because of this gesture. This man played with my feelings, thought I was just a body at his disposal, and deceived me with this contract.

I may love him, but I don't know if it's because of our pleasurable relationship in bed or because he's affectionate at times.

But what about day-to-day life?

Do I truly love Fazza?

Do I want him in my life as a present husband, even though he is controlling and possessive?

Damn it!

I must be completely insane!

How can I love the man who kept me by his side with a contract?

I hurry, getting to my room as quickly as possible. I open the door and enter, closing it behind me.

I sigh, feeling relieved to be in the comfort of my room.

"I don't think anyone will interrupt us now."

I turn my face in horror.

"What are you doing here, Samira?" I ask, heading towards the door and holding the doorknob.

"If Fazza isn't mine, he won't be anyone else's."

The woman is out of control.

"Do you love him, Samira?" I ask, hand on the doorknob.

"No, I don't love him. But I won't lower myself to be the ex-wife of the sheikh. I was born to be a real princess, and so I shall be!" she says, coming towards me.

"Sorry, Samira, but that's not an option. Maybe you should see life from another angle," I say, opening the door, quickly take out the key, and lock the door from the outside.

I look around for someone when Fazza appears with his brothers, Khalil and Omar.

"LET ME GO, SOMEONE HELP ME! THIS CRAZY WOMAN LOCKED ME IN!" Samira says, playing the victim.

"What's going on here?" Fazza asks, running his hand through his hair, disheveled.

"FAZZA, FOR ALLAH, GET ME OUT OF HERE!" Samira says, shouting.

"Why did you lock her up?"

I widen my eyes, unable to believe he asked me that question.

"You're still asking, Fazza? This crazy woman came after me again."

"SHE'S LYING. LIAR! SHE SCRATCHED ME ALL OVER. OPEN THE DOOR AND YOU'LL SEE WHAT SHE DID TO ME."

Impatient, I hand the key to Fazza, who takes it and opens the door while I keep a certain distance.

Through the door, Samira exits with her arms and face scratched, without her hijab, and her hair disheveled.

"This crazy woman attacked me and tried to lock me in her room," she says through fake tears.

"Fazza?" I call his name, seeing confusion in his eyes. "Are you going to believe her? I don't believe it" My eyes fill with tears "Maybe it's better if we get a divorce, give me freedom..."

I quickly place my hand on my stomach, feeling a sharp pain.

"Helena?"

It's the last thing I hear before I faint.

Fazza

HOURS LATER...

WHEN I see that Helena's condition is stable, I go into my office and order them to call Samira.

I sit in an armchair, feeling the velvet carpet beneath my fingers, and close my eyes for a few seconds. The door to my office is flung open, and without even asking for permission, Samira storms in, out of control.

"I hope this Helena takes her rightful place," my ex-wife says as if I had gone back on what I said.

"Samira," I say her name, taking a deep breath. "Your belongings will be sent to your father's house. I've already called and informed him that you're on your way."

"W... what?" she stammers.

"I don't go back on anything I say. As for our daughter, since she is still a newborn, I will let you take her. But later, I want Aysha back in my palace."

Samira starts pacing back and forth, clearly losing control.

"I don't want that girl! I don't want anything that reminds me of you. I hate you, Fazza, I HATE YOU!"

Samira begins to scream, causing me to close my eyes tightly.

I don't have the patience for this.

I open my eyes and see employees entering my office in response to the screaming.

"Aysha will not set foot outside this house, but I can't say the same for you, Samira."

I order my staff to remove Samira from my office. Once she is removed, I ask them to light a hookah and leave me alone, as I need to clear my mind.

CHAPTER THIRTY-THREE

Helena

"*She is pregnant, for Allah's sake.*"

I hear Aiyra's whisper beside me and squeeze my eyelids shut. I open my eyes with difficulty and see a room with a white ceiling, quickly recognizing it as my own.

I turn my face to the side and see Fazza looking at me while scratching his black beard.

"Sweetheart, you're awake." Aiyra comes towards me.

"How did I end up here?" I feel a sharp sting in my hand and see a needle with an IV drip.

"The doctor said you're very weak and overwhelmed, which isn't good for the babies," Aiyra says in a sweet voice.

"How long have I been here?" I ask, feeling dizzy.

"One day, my dear."

Fazza approaches with his hand in the pocket of his beige shorts; he looks almost like a *playboy* with his *look*.

I want to sit up, but my back hurts, so I close my eyes slowly and then open them again.

"How are the babies?" I ask, wanting to know if there are any updates.

"The doctor listened to their hearts and said they're fine; you just need to take better care of yourself."

I nod, raising my eyes again, and find Fazza with a serious expression and a furrowed brow.

I look at the needle in my arm and, impatiently, pull it out, then press the spot hard to stop the bleeding.

"I hate these things," I murmur, seeing my mother-in-law's admiring look.

"It's alright," Aiyra says, as if she were trying to normalize the situation.

"Give me something to eat, just don't poke me again." Once I see the bleeding has stopped, I sit up on the bed.

I look towards the door when someone knocks and blink a few times upon seeing my sister and mother walk through it.

"Helena Carolina Simões, tell me you're eating well. Do I need to feed you myself like I did when you moved in with us?" Mom bursts in like a whirlwind, giving me one of her lectures.

I can't contain my smile, and my eyes shine with the joy of seeing them.

Fernanda jumps onto the bed.

"You little troublemaker, trying to give us a heart attack?" Nanda says amid the hug while I smell her neck.

"What an exaggeration," I murmur.

Fernanda stands up, staying by my side while Mom kisses the top of my head.

"So this is the man who had the audacity to marry my daughter and didn't even come to my house to ask for her hand in marriage?" Mom says with disapproval.

"Mom," I murmur, rolling my eyes.

I lift my face towards my mother-in-law and Fazza.

"Fazza, Aiyra, this is my sister, Fernanda, and my mother, Solange," I say in their language.

I'm surprised to hear Fazza speaking halting Portuguese and must admit that the accent sounds perfect with his voice.

"It's a pleasure, sorry about the permission part."

The sheikh circles the bed with graceful steps.

My mother is caught off guard when he takes her extended hand and kisses it, then does the same with the other, ending with a kiss on the forehead in a gesture of respect.

"Don't be fooled by appearances," I murmur to my family.

Fazza gives me a deadly look, which I'm not afraid of.

My husband greets Fernanda.

"I see things are pretty heated around here," Nanda teases. "He's even more handsome in person than in the photo, sheikh. I'd give anything to see Vitória's reaction when she finds out you married a sheikh, sis, especially an emir. That bitter woman who used to laugh at you."

I roll my eyes, remembering my "classmate."

Fazza raises an eyebrow, and I'm grateful that my mother-in-law doesn't understand what we're talking about.

"Fernanda..." I make a face. "No details."

"Oh, really?"

I shake my head.

"I thought he already knew."

"Partially." I shrug. "Now tell me, how did you end up here out of the blue?" I want to change the subject.

"It wasn't out of the blue. Your husband called us and asked for our company; it seems things aren't going too well here." Solange crosses her arms, giving Fazza a dirty look.

"This is my cue to leave. I'll let you ladies talk, I have pending matters to attend to." The sheikh makes an excuse and leaves the room with his mother, who has a radiant smile in her eyes.

I am left alone with Mom and my sister, who soon sit on the bed.

"Wow, this man is really on your case, sis."

I lie down on the bed, closing my eyes.

"Yeah, but given everything that's happened, I don't know what to think anymore," I murmur without opening my eyes.

"I think a good talk between you two would be best," my mother says.

"Now tell me you're going to stay here with me for a while?"

"We can't, dear, we're only staying for two days. But if it were up to your sheikh, we'd be living here with you. Can you believe he even asked how much we would want to live in the palace, all for your sake?" Mom says proudly.

Little does she know everything I've been through at his hands.

I ENTER THE DINING room with Mom and Nanda, who were invited to join us at the table.

I confess that the first thing I did was look for Samira, but she's not here.

Has she left?

We three sit down, and I take a seat next to Fazza, who sits at the head of the table.

"I hope you're enjoying your stay," Fazza says solicitously.

"Yes, we are," Mom replies.

"Tomorrow we could go shopping, sister," Nanda comments excitedly. "You can show us around, Helena."

I make a face and think Fazza notices that I'm not too keen on going out.

"If you prefer, I can ask Isa to accompany you. Helena isn't in a condition to go out in the hot sun."

I wanted to say I'd go just to contradict him, but I force myself to agree.

"You'll love Isa; she's excellent. And don't stay cooped up here for my sake; go explore Agu Dhami, after all, it's not every day you two leave Brazil," I conclude, seeing the first course being served.

We all eat in a mild atmosphere, as if nothing had happened, with the languages mixing, Portuguese with Arabic.

I see Safira enter the room, call the little girl, and hold her tiny hand.

"This is Safira, I told you about her."

My sister is enchanted by the girl's beauty and how she wears expensive jewelry.

Just as I was amazed when I first moved to the palace, Mom and Nanda are too.

CHAPTER THIRTY-FOUR

Helena

I **tap** my hand beside the bed, realizing that I must have slept too long and now I can't fall asleep.

Mom and Nanda are in the adjacent wing, sleeping in rooms reserved for them.

I sit on the bed, looking around.

My mind drifts to the sheikh.

Is he in his room?

I close my eyes, internally debating whether to go to his room or not.

Amid my indecision, I get out of bed, grab a hijab, and leave my room.

I walk slowly, my feet dragging on the floor, guiding me towards his room.

The door is closed, and through the crack underneath, I can see a faint light on. I stop near the door, putting my ear to it to try to hear something, but it's all silent.

I stand there for long seconds, straining to hear anything.

I must be crazy for being here.

I sigh, pulling my ear away from the door.

"Helena?"

I hear Fazza's deep voice from the other side of the room.

I clench my hand tightly, wondering whether to enter the room or run away.

Opting for the easier choice, I decide to run away.

I take a few steps until I hear the door open, I don't turn around and continue walking until I feel his firm hand on my arm.

"What are you doing here?" he asks, making me glance at him over my shoulder.

"I don't know..." I murmur.

"Do you want to come in?" Fazza doesn't let go of my arm. "I think I owe you an explanation."

I look at him for long seconds until I finally agree.

My husband doesn't say anything, just guides me into his room.

He goes to his bed while the door closes behind us.

Fazza picks up an open notebook from the sheets and closes it, setting it aside.

His bare chest contrasts sharply with the dim light of the room.

"Sit down," he says as a command.

"I'm fine standing, I don't trust myself around you."

"Stop being stubborn, woman. I'm just asking you to sit."

"And stop being bossy," I retort defensively.

"Helena, damn it! Sit down, I'm tired of arguing with you."

I huff at his words.

Against my will, I stomp my feet on the floor and sit on the bed.

"Are you happy now?" I ask, forcing a smile.

Fazza looks at me for long seconds, as if he's about to strangle me given the circumstances.

"Now it's better. I believe it didn't hurt to do what I asked."

I don't say anything.

The sheikh moves closer, his knee very close to mine.

I hold my hands together.

"Helena..." Fazza releases a heavy breath before he begins to speak. "I didn't suspect you yesterday; I just saw Samira's current state and chose to agree with her, making her stop that little show."

"And, in return, you chose to hurt me," I interrupt.

"Let me finish speaking!" Fazza narrows his eagle eyes. "I didn't mean to hurt you; I just want all this madness to end. I'm sorry if I hurt you; it wasn't my intention. Sometimes I forget that my words deeply wound you."

"And now what are your plans?" I ask, fearing the answer.

"Since you told me you were pregnant, my plans have gone up in smoke. I no longer have control of the situation. I, who have always had everything under control, see my home burning down in all this confusion, confusion that I caused," he says desperately.

"Confusion started the moment you brought me into your life. Did you do the right thing, Fazza?"

We stare at each other for long seconds.

"Never say you were a mistake in my life, and I understand that's what you're implying. Of all the craziness I've done in my life, you were the best of it, Helena." He tries to hold my hand, but I pull it away.

"When will all this end?" he asks with a melancholic voice.

"When I feel ready for you. Who guarantees that you won't get bored and look for another wife?"

"I won't do that, I want you more than anything in this life. When Samira was in my bed, all I saw in front of me was you. Like an angel, you were on my mind. I want you every night sharing the same bed as me."

I need to be resistant, but it's difficult with him saying all these things.

I get up from the bed, but Fazza is faster, grabbing my hand and pulling me onto his lap. I clutch his chest, losing my balance, and sit between his legs.

I don't try to struggle because I know it's in vain, as he holds my waist tightly.

"Why all this reluctance? Where is that captivating woman I married?" he murmurs, removing the hijab from my head.

"You made me this way." I lift my eyes to his face.

"And just as I made you this way, I will make you return to the enchanting woman I married. Not that you aren't now. I curse myself every day that I wake up without you by my side."

"Consequences of life," I murmur.

My husband moves easily, laying me on the bed and mounting over my body.

"Let me be only yours, Helena. Just be mine. I give you my word that I will never find another wife, and if words aren't enough, I will prove to you every day that I am worthy of you."

I blink a few times, not ready for this, not ready to hear his declarations.

"Will you sleep with me tonight?" Fazza asks, lowering his chest and sniffing my neck.

"Just sleep?" I ask with a choked voice.

"Unless you desire something more."

His hoarse voice near my ear makes me shiver.

"Then let's just sleep..."

I admit that I don't know if I can resist his advances.

CHAPTER THIRTY-FIVE

Fazza

I lie beside my wife, propped up on my elbow, looking into her eyes.

I may be everything she said, but I love her. I love her to the point of divorcing all my other wives just for her, just to see a radiant smile on her lips, to spend all my time with her.

When I'm next to Helena, nothing else matters.

Only her, just her.

I stroke her face, watching her close her eyes gently.

"Fazza..." she murmurs my name.

"Tell me, my princess."

"You said we were just going to sleep."

I can't help but smile at her refusal.

"And am I doing anything?"

Helena opens her eyelids, looking at me sideways.

"Take off your tunic and lie closer to me," I ask, seeing her roll her eyes.

My wife gets up, removes her tunic, leaving only her panties and bra.

Her skin is so perfect it makes me want to touch her, smell her, kiss every little bit of her.

Damn, how I miss her!

I pull her body closer to mine, aligning her back against my chest. My hand caresses her belly where the fruit of our love grows.

"I was a fool when I refused to have a child with you. Today I see that it's all I've ever wanted..." I say near her ear, nibbling on her earlobe, watching her body shiver.

"It's hard to step out of your comfort zone, isn't it, my sheikh?" Helena's voice is husky.

I try to make the most of the situation, sliding my hand down the waistband of her panties, tracing down to the center of her pleasure.

"Fazza..." she whines.

"Tell me you don't want this, and I'll stop."

Helena sighs.

My hand enters her panties, my fingers feeling her warm skin, craving my touch.

"Please..."

Helena can't speak.

"Let me taste this little pussy?" I ask, lying on top of her.

"You said we were just going to sleep."

There's so much excitement in her voice that I could come just from her tone.

"I changed my mind." I give my best smile.

I lower my face, joining our lips in a slow, tender kiss. I suck on her tongue, and my sweet princess surrenders to the kiss.

I lower my face and squeeze her breast over her bra with force.

"So tasty..." I let slip as I kiss her belly. "You will be the best mother our children could have."

I raise my face and see her eyes shine.

I easily tear the thin fabric of her panties, too impatient to slide them down her legs.

Helena bends her legs, spreading them wide for me, and her intimacy glows with excitement. I run my finger through her wetness, her nectar providing the best feeling of possession inside me.

Without wasting time, I take her, bringing my face close, sucking her pussy hard, taking her folds with my beard scratching her sensitive skin.

My wife begins to writhe on my mouth, and with my free hand, I move up to her breast, squeezing it tightly.

I insert two fingers inside her and suck with force and desire, watching her writhe beneath me. Helena's delicate fingers press into my hair, holding me there. Her grip is strong, showing that she is at the peak of her desire.

Soon I feel her walls clenching around my fingers, I pull my hand from her ass, pushing my tongue deep into her pussy, sucking everything out of her.

I'm crazy in love with this woman.

"Fazza, oh, heavens..." she moans, biting her lip.

I lift my face and see her relaxed expression of pleasure.

"Does my wife feel sleepy now?" I ask, watching her yawn.

"Too much, husband."

Her voice is the most beautiful melody I love to hear.

"Then come, let's sleep." I pull her body closer to mine.

I try to ignore my aching desire and focus only on my sweet wife.

I MUST BE IN THE BEST dream of my life...

What the hell is happening?

I open my eyes, seeing my goddess riding on my lap.

How did I not feel this before?

How did I not see her stimulating me?

How did Helena manage to bring me to this peak of desire?

"Fuck, Helena..." I say with a hoarse voice. "The pregnancy... Our children..."

I hold onto her waist, unable to control myself in the face of the woman moving on my member.

"They are fine, let me make you come, husband." She bites the corner of her lip.

Her long wavy hair falls over her shoulder, making me see the goddess I have on top of me.

I can't resist; I don't know how long she's been there, claiming me as hers.

I pull her lips to mine and devour her mouth with lust, pushing my cock deeper into her pussy.

It doesn't take long for me to come, hard, thrusting one last time inside her while sucking her lip forcefully.

Helena quickly follows and writhes.

I feel her walls pulsing around my penis.

We collapse exhausted on the bed, my wife lying on top of me.

"What are you going to do today?" I ask, caressing her face.

"Nanda and mom are going to the mall with Isa, so I'm not sure what I'll do."

Her green eyes pierce me to the soul.

"While they are out, come with me. I have to go to the opening of a factory; I swear I won't make you uncomfortable, and you won't have to walk much," I ask, wanting her company.

My day is going to be a complete bore, and maybe with Helena by my side, it will be more exciting.

"Alright, that's fine. And what should I wear?" she asks excitedly.

"I'll ask my mother to help you; I'm not very good at that. But remember, you are now the only wife of the sheikh, the most powerful woman in the United Arab Emirates, so always dress accordingly. Any misstep reflects on my entire family and now your family as well." I take her lips in a calm and slow kiss, with our tongues meeting in a sensual embrace.

CHAPTER THIRTY-SIX

Helena

I **gaze** admiringly at my husband, who concludes his speech before his people, who applaud him. He makes a small gesture of thanks with his head.

I can't contain my smile when he glances sideways and our eyes briefly meet.

I remain in the same spot as Fazza moves away from the microphone, heading towards the people waiting behind the protective barrier.

I take a few steps and see some men shaking Fazza's hand with admiration.

The sheikh's white tunic contrasts with the golden details of the accessories hanging from his neck. An *Igal* on his head shields him from the scorching sun of Agu Dhami, giving him a more serious appearance.

My husband listens to each person who starts a conversation with him, being attentive to his people.

For the first time, I see Fazza performing one of his duties outside the palace, and it's as if he was born to do this; his ease is enviable.

I lift my gaze and observe the factory behind me. An imposing building that Fazza came to inaugurate and give his final word as emir, blessing the place with prosperity for the Emirate.

After a few minutes, he says goodbye and comes toward me.

"So?" His voice is muffled as he is handed a glass of water.

"I enjoyed seeing my husband in action," I murmur, remembering that I can't show affection in public.

Sometimes I have to control myself from kissing him when we're not in our room.

Fazza finishes his water and hands the glass to one of his men.

"Shall we go? I need to stop by the mosque."

I agree and walk by his side.

We approach the cars waiting for us.

"SHEIKH?" I CALL MY husband, who is seated in his office chair.

"What do you want, Helena?" He raises his gaze from the notebook towards me.

I look at Nain, who is observing everything attentively.

"How do you envision our future? I mean as your wife. Do you see me raising our children until my death?"

I see Nain's eyes widen briefly.

"Death is a strong word. I don't know what to expect from our future. I don't know why I'm still surprised by your questions..." The sheikh lets out a smile.

"I don't want to spend the rest of my days being the perfect wife who only knows how to take care of the children. I want to be useful in some way," I continue, drawing the attention of the two men.

"What do you have in mind?" My husband closes the notebook, placing his hands together on the table.

I see the ring gleaming on his finger.

"I'm not sure. I know I can't get involved in your business, but isn't there something I could be involved in? Like an NGO or some cause related to women in your country, helping with education. We know that women's education in the UAE is still very challenging..."

Fazza remains silent, and I feel anxious as he lifts his head, meeting the eyes of his advisor, Nain.

"Nothing is stopping you, Emir, as long as it's all within our laws."

I sigh upon hearing Nain speak.

My husband looks back at me, and his eyes linger on my face for long seconds.

"If that's what you want, then fine. But remember, do everything with my approval first; don't take any action without my knowledge."

I let out a smile of happiness.

"Of course you would find a way to control my actions; if you didn't, it wouldn't be you," I murmur, seeing him curl his lip to the side. "It's better than nothing. I'm not complaining, thank you."

"If you have any questions, talk to Lâmia, Khalil's mother. She has some organizations that might interest you."

"Why didn't I know about this before?" I cross my arms, looking at my husband.

Fazza shrugs.

"Perhaps because that house is always so full, and you never had the chance to talk."

Lâmia always has breakfast with us, and that's the only time of day I see her. I've always been impressed by the fact that she and Aiyra get along well, even though they shared the same man.

Maybe this is the essence of a polygamous marriage, something I'm not ready to face.

Now that I have Fazza all to myself, I won't allow a third person to come in.

Fazza's father had several wives, but in the end, he had only two of them, leaving them widowed very early.

IN THE SHEIKH'S GRASP

I ENTER THE ROOM AND see my sister and mother seated. Khalil is speaking in Portuguese with them.

"Sorry, I took a while to come back," I say, joining my husband.

"It's okay, dear, this young man was telling us about the palace. Did you know that the wall details are made of real gold?"

My mother has a funny expression on her face, as if what she heard was madness.

"I know, Mom," I murmur, smiling.

"Mrs. Solange, gold has never been a problem for us," my husband boasts, sitting in the armchair and crossing his feet.

"Alright, dear," Mom mocks.

Fazza bursts into laughter, finding it amusing.

"What's so funny about it if it can't even be shown?" my sister asks, raising an eyebrow.

"I don't need to go around showing it, but I enjoy a life of comfort and being able to provide my family with the best money can buy. To give them all the gold they need. See the necklace on your sister's neck? Now tell me, what haven't we shown? My princess is the most beautiful in this Emirate and wears the most expensive jewels." He frowns.

"And what about that scarf on her head? Why cover her beauty?" my sister questions my husband.

Just as I'm about to intervene, Fazza speaks again:

"Because her physical beauty is only mine. Helena belongs to me, just as her hair is only mine. I can't afford to let another man steal her from me. Besides the customs of my religion, which I'm not in the mood to discuss..."

My sister seems about to speak, but Fazza cuts her off:

"My house, my rules, topic closed. Don't argue about something that won't lead anywhere; for your sister's sake, let's change the subject," he says calmly.

For everyone's sake, Khalil changes the subject.

CHAPTER THIRTY-SEVEN

Helena

A FEW MONTHS LATER...

I **hear** little Aysha crying. Since Samira left, she hasn't bothered to check on her daughter, leaving the child in the sheikh's care.

I enter the little girl's solitary room.

"Is everything okay?" I ask the nanny.

"Yes, ma'am. She's just a bit fussy, her teeth are coming in."

I walk over to them and ask to hold the baby.

My growing belly is a bit uncomfortable, so I adjust the girl in my arms in a way that doesn't put pressure on the twins.

"I'll take her for a walk." I smile at the nanny as I leave the room.

At first, I was hesitant to get close to the girl, afraid of what others might say, but as soon as I looked at her perfect little face, I melted.

I go down the stairs and enter the living room, where everyone is gathered.

"Helena, you shouldn't be carrying heavy things," Fazza says, coming towards me and taking our daughter from my arms.

"I don't have any medical prescription telling me not to hold cute babies. — I caress Aysha's cheek as she babbles something, putting her hand in her mouth and drooling on her father.

I smile seeing the mess the girl makes on her father and grab a cloth to wipe her little mouth.

"Where's her nanny? Why is she with her?" Fazza asks casually.

"She's in the room, I asked her to bring her here." My voice is high-pitched as if I'm talking to the baby.

Fazza signals for us to sit, and my eyes meet those of my mother-in-law.

It's amazing how drastically she has changed.

Not that I'm complaining; I'm loving these months with my husband and his family, or as he says, our family.

"You know what I was thinking," I say, holding Aysha's chubby little hand while Fazza strokes her black hair.

"You and your ideas." My husband rolls his eyes briefly.

"Let her speak, dear," Aiyra interrupts him, making her son quiet.

"This time it's nothing extravagant, just something simple." I lift my face to meet my husband's dark eyes. I want to touch his face, but I restrain myself. "We could have Aysha sleep with her sisters. Why does she need to be in a separate room when her sisters are in the same environment? I believe it's better if they grow up together, so there's no rivalry between them."

I feel Fazza's hand hold mine that's resting on the sofa. His grip is restrained, firm, as if thanking me for treating his daughters well.

"I think it's a great idea." My mother-in-law's eyes shine with joy. "And you, son, what do you think?"

"I have to agree that it's a great idea, one of the few that I didn't have to think about before answering." The sheikh lets out a laugh.

I know that in recent weeks I've been driving Fazza a bit crazy with my ideas for changes.

But what can I do if I'm feeling bored?

Carrying twins isn't easy, especially now in the final trimester when my belly leaves me breathless, and I need to pee every ten minutes.

Khalil's mother had to travel, and when she returns, she will update me on her NGOs. Lâmia was very pleased to know that I intend to continue her work with Muslim women.

I SMOOTH MY BELLY OVER the smooth fabric of my nightgown, while I leave my phone on the dresser after ending my call with Mom.

Solange and Fernanda are excited about the twins' birth and eager to return to Agu Dhami.

I miss them a lot and understand that they live so far away, but my longing doesn't understand that. Fazza has already invited them to live here, but they refused. Maybe now that Nanda is single, she might accept to come live here.

"Can I know what my wife is thinking?"

I lift my face and see Fazza walking toward me, wearing only boxer briefs, with his legs exposed and his chest bare with a few hairs.

I bite the corner of my mouth.

"I'm just daydreaming, nothing important."

The Sheikh stops in front of me and holds my waist.

"How do you manage to get even more beautiful every day?"

I can't help but smile.

"You're saying that just to cheer me up because I'm far from being beautiful with this big belly and swollen feet." I roll my eyes.

"Come here, let me massage your feet." My husband winks seductively.

With ease, he lifts me onto his lap, laying me down on his bed, or rather, our bed. Since the day we got together, we haven't stopped sleeping together.

His lips touch mine in a quick kiss, one hand resting on my belly while the other lifts the fabric, caressing my skin.

My body tingles from the cold touch of his ring.

"My little men..." He lowers his face, kissing my belly. "I love seeing your mother's curves, but it's time for you to come out, if you understand what I mean, Daddy here *wants* to enjoy her."

I can't contain my laughter and laugh out loud.

"Emir, you're so interested, stop trying to persuade our children." I squeeze his hair, making his beard brush against my belly.

Soon our boys wake up and start moving according to what their father says.

Fazza decided that we won't have sex until our children are born, not that I don't tease him occasionally, or that we don't exchange affection in other ways without penetration.

"I'm crazy to bury myself in that hot little pussy. I'll need a whole week for how hard I'm going to fuck you." He raises his lust-filled eyes in my direction.

"Sheikh, please, don't start." I murmur, feeling my intimacy throb for him.

"I love the way you look at me. I love your innocence in the face of everything I can give you. I love every detail of your body. I can't go a single day without seeing your face light up my day. If you ask me what love is, I'll answer that love is loving the most charming woman, a crazy fan who completely changed my life. I love you, Helena. And I love you even more for having my daughters as yours and for carrying in your womb the future emir of Agu Dhami. How could I live in a world where you're not? How did I spend so much time without you?"

My eyes overflow with tears; if his intention was to bring out my hormones, he succeeded. I've always waited for these words, and now I can't stop crying.

"Oh, my sheikh..." Words fail me and a sob of happiness escapes my throat.

Fazza approaches, wiping my tears while laughing. The loud sound of his laughter echoes in our room.

"Don't laugh, I'm a pregnant woman about to explode, and you come at me with these words..."

"What, didn't you like it?" His forehead furrows, making me smile.

"Of course I liked it, but... but..." I blow my nose loudly, my hormones peaking and falling. "I also love you and wanted to say beautiful words to you, but I'm terrible at it." I hold his face and caress it. "How I love you, Fazza. I never imagined I'd marry a sheikh; despite my fascination, it was just a distant dream. But now I'm here, completely and unconditionally in love with the most possessive and controlling sheikh."

My husband briefly closes his eyes and then opens them, filled with tenderness and passion.

"Know that I am possessive, yes, and I take care of what is mine. Helena, you are mine, only mine. Your body is all mine, and of course, our boys for a short while. But in the end, you will always be mine!"

CHAPTER THIRTY-EIGHT

Helena

I **feel** a slight pressure in my belly and squeeze my eyelids as I feel a contraction; it must be just another practice one.

I lie on my side, contorting.

"Is everything okay, my love?"

I smile when I hear Fazza calling me and open my eyes, meeting his intense black eyes.

"Contractions," I whisper, forcing a smile.

"Are they rhythmic? Can you count them, or do you want me to count?"

"Not rhythmic yet, you can go; I'm fine." I gesture for him to leave.

"Are you going to stay here alone?"

"Any problem?" I raise an eyebrow, feeling heavy with these babies inside me.

"I don't like leaving you alone." Fazza puts a knee on the bed, planting a kiss on my forehead.

"I'm not up to getting out of this bed." I huff, smoothing my huge belly.

"I'll ask Mom to check on you from time to time. I'll be working here at the palace; I don't want to be far away."

I close my eyes in agreement and hear the sound of his footsteps, indicating he is leaving the room.

I FEEL SWEAT TRICKLING down my forehead, and I even think the air conditioning might be off.

With great effort, I sit up on the bed, and a strong contraction makes me groan in pain.

This time, they are more rhythmic and painful.

When I think of grabbing my phone, I hear the door open and my mother-in-law peek her head in, wanting to know if everything is okay.

"Helena, by Allah, you are sweating all over."

"I think it's time, mother-in-law..." I let the sentence trail off, lying back down on the bed in pain.

Quickly, Aiyra starts shouting in the hallway, calling for the midwife and my husband.

When they said contractions were mild, they surely weren't talking about this.

Soon the room is filling up, and my mother-in-law stays by my side.

"Helena, I'll do an examination. We'll have your delivery here, but if needed, we'll move to the hospital wing."

The doctor asks me to bend my legs, with a sheet over me to keep my modesty covered.

I feel as if I've run a marathon; my body is exhausted, and it seems like I've been having these contractions for a long time.

"Madam, you are nine centimeters dilated. If things continue this way, we'll have the babies here soon," the woman says, making me close my eyes.

I take a deep breath, and soon strong hands hold mine. I open my eyes and see my sheikh.

"Did you think I'd leave you alone?" he whispers, stroking my hair. "How are you feeling?"

"Are you really asking me that, Fazza? Do I look okay?" My voice sounds more ironic than he deserves, but the pain cutting through my body prevents me from being pleasant.

"Alright, you're right..." Fazza makes a face as he sees me squeeze his hand.

I squeeze his fingers as the contraction hits hard.

"Get ready, bring everything needed. The babies are in a hurry," the doctor says as she sees something between my legs.

"Oh, heavens, this is going to tear me apart," I curse, feeling my whole body numb as if I didn't need anesthesia.

Every muscle in my body is in agony.

I close my eyes and soon hear the doctor say:

"Don't stop, madam. Push hard and pull gently. I see the baby's head, not much left."

Fazza sits by my side and with his free hand grabs a cloth to wipe my sweat.

"You are the strongest woman I know, my princess. It's so close to having our children. My longed-for son, who came from the most unexpected woman, the one I thought would never be more than a mere..."

I squint my eyes, seeing him choose his words carefully.

"Know that I love you and that our story began in the most wrong way, but in the end, it worked out. And our children are proof of that."

"Showing feelings, sheikh?" I murmur, doing what the doctor asked. "Don't forget we're not alone; there are some women around."

Fazza lifts his face, and those around him look at him with admiration.

Of all the men in this palace, the emir is the most reserved emotionally, largely due to their culture.

I entwine my fingers with my husband's, feeling a wave of pain course through my body and with a suppressed groan, I exhale forcefully.

Soon, a baby's cry echoes through the room.

I close my eyes and a sudden fear runs through my body.

What if it's another girl?

Not that I wouldn't love her, but Fazza wants a boy so much.

The cry gets closer and when I open my eyes, my husband is already holding our baby, a small bundle in his arms.

I can't help but notice the sparkle in Fazza's eyes.

I never thought I could feel more fulfilled than this; my husband is holding our child.

The sheikh brings his mouth close to the baby's ear and whispers words into it.

Tears well up in my eyes; when I thought I had seen everything in this life, I'm even more moved by my husband whispering the Adhan into our baby's right ear.

Soon, I feel a pain run through my body, reminding me that there is still another baby inside me.

"Helena, I can already see the little head."

"By Allah, just tell me what it is soon," I plead, writhing as I see Fazza with a smile on his lips.

"You know I've never loved a child any less because of their gender," Fazza murmurs, making me believe it's a girl.

"Is it a girl?" I ask, gripping the sheet and hearing a second cry.

"Our little Mohammad." Fazza places our baby in my arms.

Clumsily, I hold my boy, and tears keep streaming down my face.

Fazza whispers the Adhan into the ear of our second baby, who is crying even louder.

"Zayn, our second boy, this one has a throat that shows what he came into this world for." He kisses the baby's forehead, not caring if it's still covered in blood.

I thought I wouldn't like the names Fazza chose, but I love them; they suit my boys perfectly.

I hold Mohammad so tightly that they have to almost beg me to let them take him to clean and return him to me so I can nurse him.

CHAPTER THIRTY-NINE

Helena

DAYS LATER...

I **place** my little Zayn in the crib; his hair, which was cut, is starting to grow back.

Mohammad sleeps in the crib beside him, while little Zayn has just fallen asleep.

I find myself lost in watching them; they are the most beautiful babies I have ever seen. It must be because they came from me, and my possessive side flares up every time I see them.

"Daughter?"

I lift my face and see my mother entering the room.

"I was distracted, sorry," I murmur, crossing my arms.

"Your husband is waiting for you in the living room. It seems that the guests have arrived."

I roll my eyes.

Fazza forgot to mention that the emir of Budai was on his way. With the birth of the twins, we ended up neglecting some duties, and it seems one of them was unavoidable.

My mother is doting on the grandchildren, and I leave the room heading toward the stairs.

Having my mother and sister here is very refreshing, especially since the mood swings still drive me crazy.

I descend one step at a time while my rings make a soft clinking sound against the metal of the handrail.

I hear male laughter coming from the living room.

I enter the room, and my presence quickly attracts the attention of some of the guests.

"Gentlemen, this is my wife, Helena Simões Al-Sabbah."

I mentally thank Fazza for coming to my rescue so quickly.

"So it was for her that the great Fazza became a one-woman man?"

My eyes catch sight of a man with a medium beard, a wicked gleam in his dark eyes, and formal clothes that highlight his tall, well-defined physique.

"Hassan," Fazza calls his name in a reprimanding tone.

"All right, my friend." Hassan places his hand on the shoulder of a woman sitting on the sofa.

I notice that the woman keeps her eyes down, fixed on the floor.

Could she be his wife?

"We have visitors?" Khalil enters, clapping his hands. "Oh, I thought it was something important."

I sense a hint of irritation in my brother-in-law's voice, and for a brief moment, I see the woman lift her face to look at Khalil.

"It's always a pleasure to see you, kid," Hassan says with a mocking tone.

I glance between the two of them.

"Funny..."

"Khalil, Hassan is my guest. We have matters to attend to, so it's best you hold your words, brother," Fazza says sternly to his brother.

"I'm aware, brother. After all, times have changed. I want to introduce my girlfriend." Khalil extends his hand to Fernanda, who is distractedly looking at her phone.

My sister looks at Khalil, confused.

Nanda doesn't speak Arabic; she understands a bit, which is why she furrows her brow.

"Take it, Nanda," I say in Portuguese, trying to help my brother-in-law with this confusion.

I lift my face, seeing a smile forming on my husband's lips.

My sister accepts Khalil's hand and stands up from the sofa, still confused.

The woman with Hassan looks at the couple in front of her with astonishment.

"Helena, I sincerely hope I won't have to kill you later," Nanda says, glaring at me.

"Great, a good relationship for you, Khalil." Hassan's voice drips with mockery.

I don't even know him, but I already dislike him.

Soon Khalil leaves the room with my sister.

We sit on the sofa facing the other couple.

I feel some eyes on me from the men accompanying Hassan.

"How is the marriage going?" Fazza asks the emir of Budai.

"Couldn't be better."

That's not what the woman beside him's gaze suggests.

The conversation that follows is rather dull, and I barely pay attention.

"SO, ARE YOU GOING TO tell me what happened in the living room today?" I ask, pulling the blanket and watching my husband do the same on the other side of the bed.

"It's a long and boring story. But Hassan is an emir, and he has my respect, just as I have his."

"Oh, come on, Fazza, you can tell me," I plead, sighing as I sit up on the bed.

"I knew you wouldn't be satisfied with that." He smiles as he pulls me into his arms, making me sit on his lap. "Malika and Khalil had an affair, something that almost led to an engagement. You know our relationships aren't like what you're used to; they'd been getting to know each other better for a few months until she broke it off. No one understood why, since they seemed to like each other. That is, until she showed up with a wedding planned with Hassan. According to rumors, her father sold her." He shrugs.

"How awful. I thought arranged marriages without the woman's consent were forbidden."

"No one knows if she didn't consent." He holds my hair in his hand.

"Of course she didn't. Did you see her face?"

"The only thing I noticed was the look from Hassan's men at my wife. These vultures, even with you in a hijab, dare to look at my wife."

I tilt my head back as I feel his lips on my neck.

"Now, about Hassan and Malika, don't get involved, my love. They know what they're doing, especially since I have a union with his Emirate. So just put it out of your mind."

"I'll try, but I admit her look left me with a nagging feeling."

"Don't interfere, Helena. Learn that in a sheikh's business, no one dares to speak out..."

"Especially not a woman," I murmur with disgust.

Fazza doesn't say anything, just continues to plant kisses on my neck.

"Let's not let this interfere with us, my sweet, perfect, and delicious one." His beard tickles my skin.

"Sheikh," I call out amid my laughter.

"How much longer until I can bury myself in this little pussy of yours?"

His voice is a whisper in my ear.

"Oh..." A moan escapes my throat. "There's still time, husband, so it's better to stick to the original plan, which is to sleep. Soon, I need to wake up to feed our boys."

"At least someone's getting some attention."

I can't hold back my laughter due to the pout he makes.

"Mohammad and Zayn are the only lucky ones in this situation."

I give him a playful punch on the shoulder and snuggle up to him.

CHAPTER FORTY

Fazza

I **step** out of the closet, find the room empty, and smile.

Helena doesn't let go of our boys.

I don't blame her, because if I could, I would spend most of my days with all my children.

I button the last button on my shirt and leave the room.

The children's room is next to ours.

I gently push open the door and see my wife sitting in the armchair with one of the twins in her arms.

"I see I've been abandoned once again," I murmur, and she lifts her face.

I walk over to Helena and sit down beside the armchair.

"I've already fed Zayn; now it's Mohammad's turn. Then we're free."

Helena brings her face close to mine, and I give her a quick kiss on the lips.

"Hassan is leaving today. I just need to sort out some matters with him, but I'll be back at the palace soon," I whisper, gently stroking our baby's head as he sucks at his mother's breast.

"Dear, you don't have to put your life on hold for us. We're fine. Not that I'm dismissing your company; far from it, I love having you around every day. But we know your duty is to your people."

My eyes meet her beautiful green ones.

Our other son grumbles, and I get up to fetch him. I stop by the crib, carefully pick up my little one, and lay him against my chest.

"You lose all your tough guy attitude with a baby in your arms," she teases as she sees me with our son.

"Are you mocking your sheikh, wife?" I squint my eyes at her. "You know I could still give you a spanking."

"Depending on the occasion, I'd love that."

I can't help but imagine her naked, her beautiful bottom presented to me.

"We'd better change the subject; I've been without sex for too long, and any vivid imagination leaves my cock frustrated."

Helena gives me one of her best mischievous smiles.

"You know I'm frustrated too, don't you?"

Our conversation is interrupted by loud laughter coming from outside the room. Soon, my daughters burst in like two little hurricanes.

"Daddy!"

Layla runs towards me, and I crouch down to let her see her brother.

Safira goes to Helena's side as the nanny places Jamile on the floor.

My other baby joins the room when the nanny brings her in.

My four girls and my two boys, all together in the same room.

"You know I want more children, don't you, Helena?" I ask my wife.

"Isn't six a considerable number, husband?" She frowns.

"Ten is a considerable number." I wink at her.

"Keep dreaming, sheikh," she mocks, removing our son from her breast and placing him on her shoulder to burp.

"Can I hold him?" Safira asks.

"Of course, sweetie. Sit here, and I'll hand him to you," Helena responds lovingly.

The twins' room is a complete mess, the typical uproar I love.

Seeing my family together is everything I cherish, and in this room are all the people I love the most, including my greatest love, the woman of my life, Helena.

WE ENTER THE BREAKFAST room; the clinking of cutlery is soft, and no one speaks, as if the atmosphere is heavy.

I spot Fernanda sitting next to my brother; of course, she already knows about Khalil's scheme and remains steadfast, supporting him.

I pull out a chair for my wife to sit next to me, then pull mine to the end of the table.

"Good morning, everyone."

"I thought you'd forgotten the most important meal," Omar mocks in a way I don't like.

I feel like kicking my older brother out of the palace, but out of respect for my mother, I keep him here.

"I was with my children." I glance sideways, winking in complicity with my wife.

"Since these twins were born, you've become such a softie, brother."

"My heart remains the same. And since when is spending time with my children wrong?" I raise an eyebrow at my brother.

Omar falls silent.

Hassan is quiet, as if he's lost all his previous day's mockery.

"Did you have a good stay, my friend?" I ask the Emir of Budai.

"Better impossible, right, Malika?"

I notice his tone is one of reproach.

The woman remains silent, her head bowed, and it's clear she has done something.

I turn my face towards Khalil, and he shrugs as if he knows nothing. My brother looks very relaxed, which makes me believe he didn't sleep alone.

He and Fernanda?

No, that's crazy, not under my roof.

I blink a few times and exhale with difficulty when I feel Helena's hand holding mine under the table, as if she were anticipating my momentary lapse in sanity.

I focus on my wife's face, and it's as if she's telling me to relax. And that's what I do, drinking my coffee calmly, chatting about random topics with the Emir of Budai, who hasn't smiled once.

I PULL MY BROTHER'S arm, making him stop in the middle of the hallway.

"What the fuck happened?" I ask, being direct.

"I don't know about the Emir of Budai, but with me..." He smiles slyly.

"Did you go to bed with Fernanda? Damn it, Khalil, you know how against this I am!" I exclaim.

"Times have changed, brother, and if you really want to know, she asked for it. Fernanda said she's trying to forget her ex-boyfriend. The man must be an idiot to leave a beautiful and fiery woman like her."

I roll my eyes, impatiently.

"At least Hassan is leaving now. And you, brother, need to find a wife; enough of this libertine life. Don't go including my sister-in-law in your conquests." I run my hand through my hair, frustrated.

"Too late, I already have. — He lets out a laugh. — And about Hassan, I stayed away from his wife just as you asked. I don't see why you're fighting with me about him."

"I know it's not your fault, but he confided in me that Malika came after you last night. He pretended not to see her leave the room and followed her, finding her outside your room with her ear to the door, where you were supposed to be with Fernanda."

"What the hell, Malika must be crazy! She should stay with Hassan; she had the choice, broke my heart, and still married the Emir of Budai. If that wasn't for greed, I don't know what is."

Khalil is about to lose his patience, so he walks away, leaving me alone in the hallway.

CHAPTER FORTY-ONE

Helena

"Finally!" I laugh as my husband lifts me up in his arms from behind. "Fazza!"

"Now you're mine, all mine. We're not leaving this room until we're completely satisfied."

The sheikh wraps his arms around my waist and lowers his lips to my neck.

"And the kids?" I ask as we walk toward the bed.

"I had a serious talk with them, and they said they'd give us a night of sex."

My body shivers as he nibbles on my ear.

"I can almost imagine that conversation," I tease, stepping away from my husband. I pull my tunic over my head, leaving me in just my panties and bra.

"Hot!" he exclaims, coming toward me.

I raise my arm, making him stop.

"First, take off your clothes; I want you naked for me," I murmur, my voice heavy with desire.

"Your wish is my command."

The sheikh starts undressing piece by piece, tossing his clothes to the floor until he stands naked before me.

I bite the corner of my lip, admiring his chest, letting my gaze travel down his defined body until it rests on his erect cock.

"Now it's your turn, get that off before I do," he says, his voice dripping with desire.

"My panties?" I ask, playing innocent.

I slowly slide the fabric down my legs, doing the same with my bra.

"So hot and so mine..."

Fazza doesn't give me a chance to say anything else; before I know it, he's lifting me onto his lap.

We lie down on the bed with his body on top of mine, and his lips claim mine. The kiss starts slow, with our tongues dancing in a languid melody.

I moan as his finger finds my pussy, slick with my desire, entering my channel.

"So hot," he murmurs between kisses.

His lips travel down my neck.

"Fazza..." I try to stop him from moving to my breast. "The milk..."

It's too late!

He squeezes, making the milk spurt onto his face. I can't hold back and burst into laughter.

"Laughing, are we, wife?" he mocks, biting my nipple without caring about the milk.

"Damn it, Fazza, don't do that again! It hurts like hell," I say, writhing on his fingers inside me.

I can't tell if it's pain from pleasure or if my nipple is just too sensitive.

"You're so hot, you don't lose your charm even with milk squirting everywhere." He grins wickedly.

"Let me ride you today," I beg with a plaintive voice.

"In that case, your wish is my command."

I sit on him, rubbing my pussy against his cock. I feel as if every part of my body is begging for this contact, for this hot sex with him.

"I won't last long the first time," he says, gripping my ass tightly.

"Same here..."

I let his cock enter my walls as I grind against him.

"It's like going to heaven." He closes his eyes briefly.

I grip his chest tightly, grinding on his cock. I bite my lips as I feel his hand slap my ass.

I thought the doctor would never clear me for sex, and now it feels like all the waiting was worth it.

My husband's face is shining with sweat, his well-trimmed beard framing his face, and his eyes locked on mine.

I don't know of a man more perfect than mine.

I'm crazy about him, mad with passion.

Fazza takes me to the peak of all my desires, leaves me frustrated, deprives me of many things, but I love him, and it feels like every second with him is worth it.

I intensify my grinding, my husband pulls me by the face, and our mouths collide in a hot, voracious kiss, igniting everything inside me.

"Grind, hot stuff... Grind, my hot stuff."

His hoarse voice leaves me numb amid our kiss.

"Damn, Helena, I'm going to come. Coming inside that pussy of yours, only yours!"

I can't hold on any longer and end up surrendering along with him.

I collapse on top of him, our breaths rapid, and silence fills the gaps in our passion.

I feel his hand gently caressing my back.

"For a brief moment, I forgot how wonderful it is to be inside you," he murmurs. "But it was so brief I almost forgot."

We smile.

"Can it ever get bad in our lives?" I ask, falling beside him.

"I don't think so. Everything with you is wonderful, and now that the palace is calm again, we'll have sex every night."

I rest my head on his shoulder, looking at his perfect face.

His chest glistens with sweat from the sex.

"It's too quiet, something will happen soon," I say, tracing my finger over him.

"Khalil needs to find a wife. Now that his sister is gone, he'll have more time to think about it." He closes his eyes thoughtfully.

"Do you have anyone in mind?"

Fernanda left and gave no hint that she ever felt anything for Khalil. I asked her, but she coldly replied no and that she would never love another man.

As for my brother-in-law, I could swear I saw him looking at Nanda with different eyes, but on this matter, I promised my husband I wouldn't interfere; they need to figure it out themselves.

"I don't have anyone in mind. We'll need to look at the single candidates and see if any attract my brother. I don't want him to enter a marriage out of obligation, with a woman he's not attracted to, if you know what I mean."

I agree, remembering Fazza's two wives. Zaya calls me almost every day or sends messages asking about her daughters. She confided in me that she's living the best phase of her life, alone, without a man to fulfill her duties as a woman.

Samira hasn't been heard from again, only that she returned to her parents' house and doesn't even want to know about her daughter. She has disowned Aysha to such an extent it's sad to see.

"Fazza, I want to start using some form of contraception. I don't want to have children right now; I want to enjoy the twins and have hot nights with my husband," I ask, and he looks at me.

"That's fine; I also want to fuck you every night."

I punch his chest, making him laugh.

"Now come here, are you ready for the next one? Because I'm just getting started."

I can't contain my laughter as I see him mount my body.

EPILOGUE

Helena

I sit on a bench under the shade of a tree, watching Fazza carry Mohammad on his shoulder while Zayn runs, stopping in front of the lion.

A few years ago, I would have thought this was crazy, until I saw how much my children love these wild animals and how you can't take away something that's already in their blood.

Zayn is the first to approach Ali, who lowers his head, and my five-year-old son hugs the huge beast.

Fazza encourages the children to share his tastes; my husband is somewhat controlling even with our kids.

I don't mind, but I know they have a great future ahead of them to govern this Emirate.

"Hi, Mom."

I glance to the side and see Aysha.

"Come sit here with me, dear." I pat her little black hair, keeping her close.

When Aysha started speaking, she saw me as a mother, especially seeing the twins with me all the time, knowing they are her siblings.

I tried various ways to contact Samira, but she refused to speak with me or even know anything about her daughter. When I gave up, I let the little girl call me Mom.

I want her to have all the love just like her siblings.

"Do you know if Jamile will be back soon?" Aysha asks.

She is almost the same age as Jamile; they grew up together doing everything in pairs.

"I don't know, Zaya hasn't sent me a message yet," I murmur, hearing Mohammad shouting to call the lion.

The three sisters went to their mother's house, and there's no forecast for their return.

"Go play with your siblings." I point out, seeing Zayn calling his sister to play.

She gets up and runs off with her dress spinning as she moves.

Fazza straightens his body and comes towards me, letting our children play among the two lions that look more like two plush bears.

"Why the frown?" I ask as my husband sits beside me.

"Remember your biological parents? I got a call last night."

I know Fazza has the contact information for the clinic where my mother is; my father died in prison about a year ago. I've never had the desire or curiosity to meet them, after all, they abandoned me.

"What about her?" I ask, seeing that he's waiting for my reaction.

"Well, she passed away; it seems she had a heart attack."

I nod, not wanting to know more.

"I sent some money so they wouldn't just throw her away."

I lift my face, and our eyes meet.

"You don't exist! You know she abandoned me, right?" I ask, being ironic.

"We must learn to forgive, my princess." He holds my hand, stroking my fingers. "I don't know which of the two will be the best candidate for Emir of Agu Dhami; I hope the right decision touches my heart."

"It will, my sheikh." I give him my best smile.

I close my eyes as I feel his hand caressing my cheek.

"Did you leave Jamal with the nanny before coming here?" Fazza asks about our youngest son.

"Your mother took him; she said she wants to spend the afternoon with him."

"I'd give her less than an hour before she hands him off to some nanny."

We laugh together.

Jamal is our youngest child, turning one year old, just in time for Fazza to plan our next child, which I've already made clear will be the last.

I know how wonderful it is to have the house full of children, but it's my body, and I want a break, so we agreed that we would have just one more pregnancy.

MY TUNIC TRAILS SOFTLY on the ground as I stand in front of the mosque, watching my husband's temple, a vast construction stretching out of sight.

It was here that I first met the sheikh when I came to his office, and he told me about the contract that united us.

It was here that I converted to Islam, becoming one of them in body and soul.

And now it will be here that I announce that I am pregnant with our next and last child. That's why I've planned a special way to tell my husband.

With great effort, I gathered all our children, from the oldest to the youngest: Safira, Layla, Jamile, Aysha, Mohammad, Zayn, and Jamal.

Our boys are now older than Jamile and Aysha, but I decided to follow the order of age.

Each of them holds a card in their hand, and Zayn is holding Jamal's hand to keep him from running off.

"Ready? Here comes your father," I say, turning my face to see my sheikh approaching with his men.

He is taken by surprise and frowns, not understanding what our children are doing there.

Next to him are Nain, Khalil, and Omar, along with a few security guards.

My husband is wearing his white tunic with a turban on his head, and his expression is serious as always.

As he approaches, I gesture for the children to put the plan into action.

A sentence forms: **"Enjoy every second, Daddy, because another little sibling is on the way."**

My husband smiles as he reads it. He rarely smiles in front of his men, but when it comes to his family, he melts and loses all his untouchable manliness.

Fazza looks at me.

"Are you pregnant?"

"Yes." I nod, unable to hold back my tears.

"My most precious diamond, I love you," he says loudly for everyone to hear.

For Fazza to show such emotion in front of others means he still loves me more than anything.

I can't contain myself and throw myself into his arms, ignoring everyone around us, feeling his wonderful scent invade my senses. It reminds me why I love this man, and we chose to give ourselves this new chance and make everything work out.

Fazza has proven every day that I am enough for his life and that we don't need a new wife.

I love that about him.

I admit that even with his controlling nature, I've adapted and learned to love him.

I love my sheikh, a dream so distant that became reality.

Now, I have a sheikh all my own, or rather, three sheiks, as Mohammad, Zayn, and Jamal are here to prove to me that it's never impossible to dream.

THE END.

Did you love *In the Sheikh's Grasp*? Then you should read *The Sheikh's Jewel* by Amara Holt!

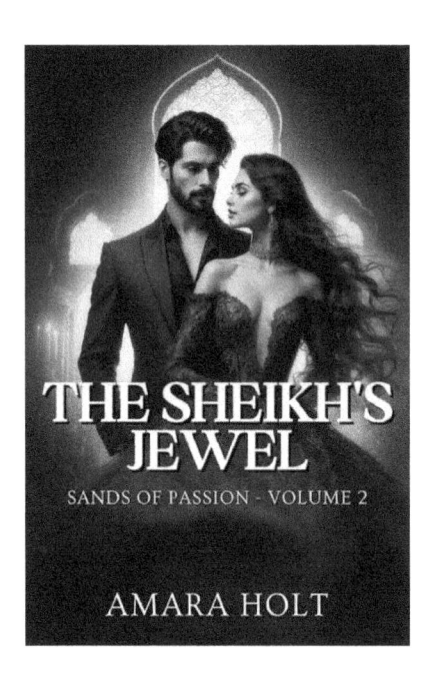

The Sheikh's Jewel: A Tale of Forbidden Desire and Unyielding Power

When the powerful Sheikh **Hassan**, ruler of the wealthiest emirate in the **Arabian Desert**, sets his sights on something, nothing can stand in his way. Known for his **ruthlessness** and determination, Hassan has never desired a wife—until the day he lays eyes on a breathtaking necklace, crafted by a renowned jeweler. But it's not the jewelry that captures his heart; it's the jeweler's stunning daughter, **Malika**.

Malika has always dreamed of marrying for **love**, her heart secretly yearning for another. But when Hassan proposes marriage without even meeting her, she is thrust into a world of **luxury**, **power**, and a man who is determined to possess her at any cost.

Torn between **duty** and **desire**, Malika faces an impossible choice: surrender to the will of a man she barely knows, or hold onto the love she thought was hers. As Hassan's **obsession** grows, so does his need to control every aspect of her life, even as he vows to protect her from all harm.

In a land where passion and tradition collide, can Malika find the strength to carve out her own **destiny**, or will she become just another **prized possession** in the Sheikh's collection?

Discover the seductive world of "The Sheikh's Jewel," where love and power intertwine in a tale of fierce desire, dark secrets, and the ultimate sacrifice.

About the Author

Amara Holt is a storyteller whose novels immerse readers in a whirlwind of suspense, action, romance and adventure. With a keen eye for detail and a talent for crafting intricate plots, Amara captivates her audience with every twist and turn. Her compelling characters and atmospheric settings transport readers to thrilling worlds where danger lurks around every corner.